THIS
LITTLE
DARK
PLACE

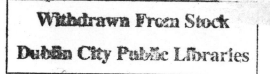

THIS
LITTLE
DARK
PLACE

A. S. HATCH

First published in Great Britain in 2019 by
Serpent's Tail,
an imprint of Profile Books Ltd
3 Holford Yard
Bevin Way
London
WC1X 9HD
www.serpentstail.com

Printed and bound in Great Britain by Clays Ltd, Elcograf S.p.A.

A complete catalogue record for this book can be obtained from the
British Library on request.

ISBN 978 1 78816 202 9
eISBN 978 1 78283 526 4

For Tarryn

I don't write this letter to put bitterness into your heart,
but to pluck it out of mine.

Oscar Wilde, *De Profundis*

CONTENTS

1

VICTORIA

August 2033

Dear Lucy,

Thank you for writing to me and for enclosing your photograph. You are as beautiful as I imagined. I have Blu-tacked you to my wall.

Before we meet – *if* we meet – I should warn you: I don't much resemble the man you may have seen in the papers. That all happened so long ago. (Has it really been sixteen years?) I'm heavier now and that thick mop of black hair is long gone. I don't want my appearance to shock you so I have enclosed a photograph of myself. I certainly don't expect to end up on *your* wall.

I have often thought about what it would be like to see you, to hear about your life, what kind of person you are, your dreams – your fears. But in my heart I never believed it could happen. I must have read your letter a dozen times and each time I open it I expect your words to have disappeared. But there they are.

I've been contacted many times over the years, by journalists, bloggers, one time a screenwriter, all wanting to know 'what really happened' in the cottage, when all they really want is for me to confirm what they've already heard. They ask about Ruby. They ask about Lanes End. They ask about the trial. I throw their letters in the bin. But you ask me a different question. You ask me to tell you 'who I really am'. And I get the feeling you truly do want to hear my side of the story.

It can't have been easy for you to reach out to me like this. I imagine you've heard a great many things about me already. I expect you've googled me. I'm so grateful you've written at all. That you ask for my version shows integrity. That you're even considering meeting me feels like a miracle. You want the facts before judging me. I cannot ask for a fairer hearing than this. So, assuming nothing, let me give them to you. Whether this serves my own ends or not, when you finish reading this letter you will know 'who I really am'. And then you can decide for yourself.

So, who am I really?

I may as well start right here with this desk. These tapered legs, the panels that fit together so neatly they form a perfectly flush surface, these wooden pegs that connect it all together. It's all my handiwork. I used to make my living crafting and selling furniture. Now I do it for the love of it. I love that each type of timber has its own smell. I love feeling, with each swipe of my block plane, smoothness replacing roughness. And the gentle sound the shavings make under my boot. And the softness of fresh sawdust.

The last couple of months I've been crafting a miniature chest of drawers for Gordon, for his wife's fiftieth. I'm reluctant to call him a friend but I suppose in a way he has become one to me. She can keep all her earrings and bracelets and loose things inside it. It's been a long time since I lived with a woman but I still remember the catastrophe of Victoria's things. Gordon and I had a good laugh about that. The last layer of French polish is drying tonight. It'll shine like a mirror.

I'm working on something for you too. A little gift. I'll give it to you if you choose to see me. You should know, though, I'm a perfectionist; if you keep me waiting too long I'll have sanded and smoothed it down so much there'll be nothing left of it. I suppose that's a bit like love isn't it? You spot things that displease you or that actively irritate you; maybe a facet doesn't glint in the light like it should or when you run your finger along an edge you feel a snag, and then you're reaching for the sandpaper and burnishing it into fine dust.

That, or you chuck it in with the offcuts and start again.

***

I met Victoria on Christmas Eve 2010 in a bar. She materialised from the crowd of swaying bodies. She sashayed up to me, a smile on her face, and draped her arms around my neck. We never spoke, it was too noisy. There was no need to. We danced. I lost track of time. I remember the lights coloured her skin alternately pink and blue. And the softness of her skin. And the smell of her hair conditioner. She was beautiful. Long straight mousey blonde hair. A couple of days after Christmas, half-naked and breathless in her parents' basement, she told me she was a dental assistant. Oh, I said, I'm a carpenter. Jesus was a carpenter, she said. And after that we were a couple.

Throughout the next year we spent every moment we could together. Victoria got to know my mother Ivy very well. They adored each other.

By the following Christmas, Victoria and I had moved out of our parents' houses and into a little semi on Beryl Avenue. Rented of course, but we loved that little house. It gave us independence. The garage was my domain, my workshop. The only bit of original furniture in that house was the oak coffee table with the magazine compartment on the side which I made for my mother and which she gave back to me when we moved in, saying it had been the only thing left to her in her mother-in-law's will. *I always despised that bitch,* she said, looking down at the coffee table as though it was her grave slowly descending into the earth. When I reminded her that I had made it for her, she just looked at me blankly. We didn't realise at the time but my mother was suffering from multi-infarct dementia and would be dead within five years.

A pleasant routine established itself in our lives. Every Sunday we drove in the van (my VW Transporter) to her parents' and then for lunch with my mother, who lived alone after the death of her second husband Frank.

We were very passionate (I hope you won't mind me mentioning) and made love often. Our relationship was everything I wanted. Victoria was so easy to get along with back then. We never fought. We never bickered. I only wanted to see her happy. And I thought we were happy.

One Saturday Victoria dragged me into a pet shop to look at the puppies and fell in love with a schnauzer.

A couple of weeks later a green van pulled up outside the house. I wasn't expecting any deliveries so paid it no mind. But then the doorbell rang.

When I collected her from work I didn't mention the mysterious package that'd been left in the back room. She squealed with delight when she saw the shrouded cage. I put my hand over her mouth and pointed to the information card the pet shop owner had provided.

Hello, my name is: Oscar

While I get used to my new home please don't make any loud noises for at least 24 hours and please don't expose me to any artificial light for a week.

Victoria threw her arms around me. Like I said, I only ever wanted to see her happy. And so her happiness was also mine.

The next morning we unveiled the cage. There he was. Plump and green. Tiny beak like a piece of chopped carrot. Eyes like two tiny black beads. An arrowhead of electric blue feathers at his rear. No bigger than a black-bird. Oscar the quaker parrot stood on his perch and tilted his head as Victoria leant in closer.

'Do you like him?' Victoria asked with her face pressed to the cage, making it seem like she was asking Oscar if *he* liked *me*.

Over the next few months Victoria taught Oscar to pick up little sticks and bob up and down and follow her finger in a circle above his head like they were dancing together. But not long after Oscar arrived he stopped coming out of his cage. And the odd time Victoria did manage to coax him out he would turn his back on her and wander off uninterestedly. One night she told me she thought Oscar was depressed and that we ought to get another one. 'He needs a companion!' she said, looking into my eyes and pressing her iPad to her heart. To me it seemed obvious what Oscar's problem was. You only had to take one look at him to see he simply didn't belong here. He had given up on life. A companion wouldn't fix him. But that was the thing about Victoria; to her there wasn't a problem that couldn't be fixed. Something wrong with your teeth? Fix them. Something wrong with your exotic bird? Fix it. Something wrong with your life? There's got to be a fix.

So we bought Alfred, another quaker, and then, one Friday morning in January 2013, Oscar was dead. Victoria wouldn't touch him. I went into the back room and approached the cage, a tea towel in my hand. Alfred was on the middle perch. Poor Oscar was on his side like a discarded toy; a fake parrot that we'd bought to entertain the real one. I buried him in the back garden.

After that Victoria lost all interest in Alfred. He was a killer, she said. Alfred the Murderous was now my responsibility.

Some new void opened in Victoria's life. Or maybe it was the same old void that Oscar had been supposed to fill. She moped. She smiled less. She googled more. Facebooked more; she started showing me pictures of infants I didn't know. Whenever she felt lost, or aimless, she dived deep into the internet like this. The iPad became attached to her hand, like an IV drip that she dragged around the house, delivering, one click at a time, a numbing drug. At night, overturned on her bedside table, a ghostly glow emanated from its edges as it received and gave out its mysterious data. And when she awoke it wasn't for me that she reached but the iPad. She'd impart the dispatches of the night to me. Pictures of celebrities. Of houses. Of appliances we didn't need. Spa treatments we couldn't afford. She was searching. Searching for something but she didn't know what. And then one night, she muted the telly and said: 'Let's have a baby.'

⁎

I write this letter slowly, carefully. I know what's at stake. Every day between one and two o'clock I go down to the library, which is always completely empty, for the peace, and I write one side of A4. Sometimes two. I can tell already it is going to be much longer than I intended. I hope you will read it to the end. When I set out to write this I knew there was a lot to cover, a life in fact, but I had forgotten how cathartic the act of setting down one's thoughts on paper is. It is just how Ruby said. As I recall these memories I relive them. In order. And so I cannot skip anything. To understand what happened in October, you need to know everything that came before. I cannot overlook even the small moments. They all matter, which is why I must write them down. When you receive this letter, when you hold it in your hands, you will feel how heavy my life is. Has been.

***

You may not know this about me, Lucy, but I'm a 'Wild' un', from a place called Wilder-on-Sea. Tucked in the northernmost tip of a jutting chin of flat coastal land west of Bowland Forest, Wilder is buffeted by vindictive westerlies off the Irish Sea year-round. It used to be a fishing town. The pubs all have names like The Anchor and The Trawler. There's one called The Mermaid's Backside. But I can't remember ever seeing a single active fishing vessel come into Wilder Marina in my life. I only ever saw them come in on Wilder Heritage Day, a yearly celebration of the town's former glory. I used to love Heritage Day. My father would park up in his Transit and get chips and we'd watch the boats come in. An old guy on a microphone would announce each boat. Old people would clap and crouch arthritically to the grandchildren in their buggies – the many grand-children of Wilder, whose parents you never saw – and point to the boats.

Once upon a time the town had flourished. With the Irish and Celtic seas to the west, the salmon- and cod-rich waters of the North Channel to the north;

Wilder-on-Sea was a fisherman's haven. There was money in Wilder. Lots of money. Houses shot up everywhere. Families moved to Wilder from all over the Northwest. There were so many children they had to build another school. But then the Common Fisheries Policy came in and almost overnight Wilder began to die. The fishing slowed to a crawl. The money dried up. Families left. Those that stayed struggled. The new school closed. Around the time I met Victoria there were hardly any young people around any more. All the jobs had moved to neighbouring towns. Now Wilder is Death's waiting room. In 2015 Wilder had one of the highest suicide rates per capita of any town in Europe. The council put up chain-link fences all along the promenade to stop people – young men mostly – throwing themselves into the sea. The whole town looked like a giant prison yard. Unless you found yourself in Wilder at birth, there was no reason to be there. 'Wild' uns' they call us: a grim badge of honour for those who choose to wear it. A symbol of endurance.

So when Victoria said 'Let's have a baby,' it came as no great surprise. In Wilder there's really not much else for a young woman to do.

Throughout 2013 we tried to conceive without success. The first nine months came and went with only a couple of late periods to show for our efforts. But she remained stoically upbeat. We carried on. We've only been trying for nine months, she said. And then nine months became a year. But still every month she clutched her hope to her chest like a lottery ticket. I loved her so much in those days. She gave me, us, direction and purpose. I wanted a child, don't get me wrong, I wanted very much to be a father, to drive my son or daughter to Wilder Marina in the Transporter and get chips and watch the boats come in on Heritage Day. But more than I wanted a child I wanted Victoria to be happy. A man can live in the isolation of a town like Wilder. He can even flourish if he doesn't need much company. But for a woman to be childless in Wilder was to become like Wilder itself, defunct and spare. Victoria and I could have been happy if we had a baby, I thought. She'd have been fulfilled and the sight of her fulfilment would have fulfilled me. But the months rolled on and gradually she began to remind me of someone who's been sat pulling the lever of the same slot machine all night waiting for the jackpot, fearing that if she walks away it might pay out on the very next pull. It became a sort of spiritual crisis for her. A trial. Via the iPad, she absorbed a whole world of half-knowledge and speculation on the pregnancy forums. The websites she read aloud from sounded almost religious. '*You will rise and you will prevail.*' '*When the night has reached its darkest point, every moment thereafter is brighter.*' They were clichés. But the words gave her hope and I didn't mind that.

On New Year's Day, four years after Victoria and I had met, we turned up at my mother's house for the traditional roast, as arranged, but she wasn't in. It was intensely cold. I called her mobile. She was at Wilder Beach, waiting for me, she said. I knew immediately something was wrong.

At the seafront the wind was biblical. The sea was very far out and the sand expanded almost to the horizon. I saw a black figure in the distance, shaped like a cross. A person with their arms stretched out. I ran to it. As I got nearer I could make out with relief my mother's coat and boots. She was leaning back into the wind with her eyes closed, an ecstatic look on her face. I was out of breath from running, and my hands went to my knees. I felt like I was bowing before her. Suddenly, the wind caught in her coat like a sail and she fell into my arms.

'Daniel?!' she shouted, the wind roaring like a rocket.

'Mum, what are you doing here?!'

'Where's your father?! He should've been here an hour ago!'

'Dad's dead, Mum!'

In the Transporter Ivy did not speak. She sat hunched over, sulking like a child as Victoria rubbed some warmth into her shoulders. As we idled at a red light, I looked down at her. She seemed so frail. So old suddenly. To my mind she was unbreakable. A woman who commanded such respect that just the sound of her weight on the creaky floorboard outside my bedroom was enough for my friends to know it was time to leave. I couldn't reconcile the Ivy in my head with this withered, beaten woman next to me. I felt ashamed. For having failed to sense her frailty. For having failed to recognise that she was not invincible, she was only a woman. Better and stronger than any man, but still human.

I took her to the GP the next morning. When the official diagnosis came through, my mother's house seemed instantly to assume an atmosphere of death. I began noticing dust everywhere, grime in the grouting, cobwebs in the corners. How had I missed this? As I cleaned it, I dredged up a montage of bittersweet memories. I'd be stood in the bathroom and suddenly I'd remember my father bathing me as a toddler, and my mother coming in with the towel and the talc and how she used to thrust the bottle forward so that the powder exploded on my belly. And I remembered how I'd sat outside their bedroom door in the middle of the night whimpering for hours. My mother told me years later how desperately she wanted to get out of bed and comfort me as I cried but my father held her in place, reminding her – correctly – that I had to grow out of it. And birthdays and Christmases and coming home from holidays to find the house was somehow smaller than we remembered. And then my father's cancer. And how much noisier the house was after he died because my mother put a radio in every room and left Radio 4 on all day.

She met Frank at my father's wake. It was held at the cricket club. Not that my father played cricket, that was just where every family function – happy or sad – seemed to be held in Wilder. I remember going outside to escape my father's over-attentive relatives and looking in through a window and seeing my mother at a table with a man sat across from her. I remember her watery smile as he talked and she listened, nodding. I remember his bushy black-and-white beard and the angular protrusion of his glasses as seen from behind. I remember him leaning across the table and taking both of my mother's hands in his.

Over the following months I saw much more of Frank. He was forever over fixing things, bringing things, food, utensils, money. I found Christian pamphlets in the kitchen drawer. *Blessed are those who mourn, for they shall be comforted.* I didn't like him from the start. One time I said as much. My mother rebuked me for being judgemental. He's just a kind lonely man, she said, he's lost someone too, just like us. Eventually, my mother came to rely on Frank for company. And then, suddenly, it 'made sense' for him to come and live with us.

He was clever. He played it perfectly. He introduced new rules into our household, small things at first – like having to wait for him to get home before eating dinner, which was sometimes late, and saying grace at table, which we never did before. Then he started implementing other rules. No soap operas for my mother. They 'rotted' her brain. No radio. If there was silence to be filled, it should be filled with contemplation and prayer. He binned my father's 'trashy' novels and replaced them on the shelf with a bible, photographs of his family (whom we never met) and religious ornaments. I'm not sure when exactly he began battering my mother.

He terrified me. Always dressed, almost clerically, in black. His neck-length salt-and-pepper hair, always dried out and bristly like his beard, made him look, to my child's eyes, like an evil king from a fairy tale.

One night, this was about a year after Frank moved in with us, I got out of bed to go to the toilet. I heard whimpering. I had grown used to the sound of my mother's nocturnal sobbing, and immediately knew that this was different. I tiptoed the length of the bungalow past the bathroom to the source of the sound. The living room door was open. Through the gap between the door and its hinges I saw the back of Frank's head above the couch, silhouetted by the light of the TV. On the screen a naked man stood over the figure of a naked woman gagged and tied to a wooden table. The man wore a Mexican wrestler's mask. The woman looked terrified of the man. She thrashed about on the table. Frank removed his glasses and placed them on the coffee table beside the couch, slowly and deliberately. He rose from the couch and moved closer to the screen. He was naked too. Too scared to move, I watched him. When his breathing began to get heavier I took the opportunity to escape back to my room where I remained, unable to sleep, all night. I held on for as long as I could but eventually I wet myself.

I suppose that was my first experience of sex.

I never slept much or well after that. Every night I dragged my chest of drawers over to block the bedroom door, as protection. Against what I wasn't sure, Frank never laid so much as a finger on me. My grades at school dipped. I was always tired. I found everyone irritating, especially teachers. One lunchtime I was hit in the backside by a football. It was an accident, and the kid who came asking for the ball back was younger than me. I picked the ball up and walked over to the kid and kicked it as hard as I could into his face. He fell to the floor. I was sent home. I'd broken the kid's nose. It was Frank who came to school to pick me up. He didn't say a word to me, nor I to him. But I sensed rage in the way he slammed the car door. That night at table he lowered his cutlery and said: *Tell your mother what you told me before.* I didn't know what he was on about, I said. *Don't lie Daniel, tell her what you said. About how you wished she'd died instead of your dad.* His voice was level, he was calm. I looked at my mother. She was white with hurt. I never said those things, I assured her. Frank closed his eyes. *But the king shall rejoice in God; every one that sweareth by him shall glory: but the mouth of them that speak lies shall be stopped,* he said. *Now look at your mother and tell her you're sorry.* I looked at her. *Say it.* I said I was sorry. *What for?* I couldn't say the words. *Daniel. What ... for?* I said I was sorry for wishing she'd died instead of my father. *There you go. Wasn't so hard was it? There may be hope for you yet,* he said. Then he picked up his fork and tucked back in to my mother's shepherd's pie.

Then there was the terrible moment in my father's old garage workshop, when I confronted Frank with a wrench. For a delicious moment the glower in his eyes gave me hope that he just might hit me back, and then my mother might've considered kicking him out. Instead he touched his fingers to the tributary of blood that had formed on his cheek, put his glasses back on and told me in a low voice that he was going to teach me a lesson.

And as the traffic lights turned green and these long-repressed memories flooded over me like the tide and my mother's tears soaked into the collar of her cardigan, I realised that Frank had made good on his vow, that he had indeed taught me an important lesson.

Over the next six months Victoria and I carried on trying to conceive. But I was preoccupied with my mother's decline. It was hard watching her trying to struggle on at home by herself.

It was around this time that Victoria's superstitions began. Egged on by the women on the pregnancy forums she started doing strange things. She stopped eating fruit. She threw out all the cleaning products and started using only vinegar and water. She put her feet in water tanks and let tiny fish eat her dead skin. She played 'songs' on her iPad that were nothing but silence but that apparently emitted an inaudible frequency that stimulated her ovaries. None of these things bothered me, until she stopped visiting my mother. One Sunday, Vic said she wasn't feeling well and preferred to stay home. I sensed a lie but didn't press her on it. She was having a rough time – we'd been trying to conceive for eighteen months then – and I thought perhaps she just needed some time to herself. But when she said she couldn't come the following Sunday I had to say something.

'I can't Dan,' she said.

'It would mean a lot to me if you came.'

'I just can't.'

'Why not?'

'Please Dan,' she said weakly. I could feel myself getting worked up. My fists clenched. I couldn't help it. I punched the cushion beside her as hard as I could. Victoria flinched, and we stared at each other for a couple of seconds in stunned silence before I stormed out.

Ivy didn't ask after Victoria that day. She seemed lost in a different time in history altogether. With just the two of us at the table, I was minded of the immediate aftermath of my father's death. The clinking of our cutlery was accompanied only by the Sunday drama on the radio.

When I got home Victoria was upstairs having a bath. She'd left her iPad on the couch. I unlocked it, the passcode was her birthday, and opened Safari. Evidently, she was a very active member on the pregnancy forums. There were various other hare-brained schemes for conceiving that she hadn't tried. Eating only seafood and spinach. Climbing into an ice bath immediately after sex. Sitting upside-down after sex. The colour orange. The list went on. And then I read something that made my stomach twist inside my body.

A thread entitled: 'IF YOU'RE TRYING TO GET PREGNANT – READ THIS!!! By Katrina, a mother of two beautiful boys.' Katrina used to work in an old persons' home. She'd been trying to get pregnant for years. She was on the brink of giving up. But then 'MDH got promoted' (I discovered MDH meant 'my darling husband'), meaning she didn't have to work any more. So she quit and after that she got pregnant straight away. Twins. What a miracle, et cetera. One day, admiring the two babies, it hit her. She knew why she had finally become pregnant. It was because she had taken herself away from death. She was no longer surrounded every day by dying people. That was the only explanation and she urged the women on the forum to 'avoid death, and places where death lurks at all costs!!!!' (this included: doctor's practices, nursing homes, funerals and graveyards), before adding: 'If someone you know is sick or dying, you mustn't see them any more. You mustn't allow their death to block the new life fighting to blossom within you.' The post had received hundreds of replies and thousands of likes. Scores of women, all using the same pseudo-religious language and shorthand, thanking her, referring to her as some sort of prophet. For the first time I felt resentful of the whole process, the whole matter. I wanted to barge in on Victoria's bath and to rage at her stupidity, at her callous, blind stupidity. Instead I went out to the workshop and spent the evening polishing an ash dining table until I was sure she'd gone to bed.

The following Sunday she said her father was in Ireland on a golf weekend and her mother had asked her to stay over, to keep her company. So on the Saturday I drove her to her parents' house, but before she got out I stopped her. I told her I knew about Katrina on the forum and why she was avoiding my mother. She said nothing. She just clenched the handles of her overnight bag tightly and pursed her lips. I had begun to feel like I knew her less and less. We sat in silence. Cars whooshed by. Seagulls twitched on the roofs of the houses. In that moment I think I experienced the first desperate pang of regret. Maybe I should have kept my mouth shut, allowed this phase to pass, just carried on trying to get her pregnant. But I felt her changing. A shell of cynicism and hardness was forming around her. I reached out to her with my hand but she avoided my touch like a cat.

Victoria announced one night that if by January we hadn't conceived she would contact the fertility clinic. We were still having sex. Mostly, perfunctory. Occasionally, aggressive. When I climbed into bed with her without a kiss or caress I did so out of love for her. I sensed her love for me was still there too, simply trapped beneath a layer of ice. Sometimes I tried melting it. Sometimes I took a pneumatic drill to it.

Christmas Day was hard. I sensed it would be my mother's last. Ivy was now living full-time in the Jerusalem Full-Time Residential Care Home. Scrawny strings of tinsel hung from each corner of the visiting room.

The nurses wore elf costumes. Some residents were arranged in a semicircle around the telly watching *It's a Wonderful Life*. Ivy didn't register me when I kissed her forehead and I knew it wasn't one of her 'good days'. I wished her a happy Christmas. I told her I loved her. I told her I was thankful for everything she'd done for me. I looked up and saw that her brow was furrowed and I thought for a moment that my words had got through, that I had stirred something deep within her.

'Do you remember too?' I said. 'It wasn't so long ago.' I squeezed her hand. I felt I had reached her. But she continued to stare straight ahead, right through me. And then I realised her expression hadn't altered at all in the time I'd been there. I followed her gaze to the window and realised she hadn't heard a single word I'd said. Her expression, which I had interpreted as recognition, was simply confusion. For it was dark and the nurses had put the lights on in the visiting room and instead of the sea, all Ivy saw was a reflection of herself in the window. Ghostly and see-through. Half there, half gone.

***

We've had a heatwave. On my walk this afternoon I got hot and sticky. I miss the Wilder wind. I used to hate it. In winter it made your fingers cold even through thick gloves. But today I longed for a blast of that coastal air.

I make sure to go for a walk every day if I can. It helps to order my thoughts. I'm not so near to the sea any more, as you know. But sometimes I see a seagull overhead and it reminds me of Wilder. You must be lost, I'll say to it, so far from the coast. And I wonder if it will ever find its way back.

**

'Zona pellucida,' Victoria said, reading from her iPad, 'is the name of the membrane that surrounds the ovum prior to implantation.' It was a dark afternoon in late January 2015. That morning she'd had her last shot of follicle-stimulating hormone before the fertilised egg was due to be transferred into her uterus the next day. 'Implantation normally occurs one to five days after the ovum has been transferred.' Victoria had read on the forums that the chances of successful implantation were increased if she stayed still. So she took a week off work and sat on the couch in orange pyjamas and watched telly. On day five I heard her leave the house and slam the door behind her. I ran to the end of the drive in time to see her turning the corner at the end of the street. I went back inside. Upstairs in the bedroom, her orange pyjamas were strewn on the floor next to the bed. I went to put them inside the laundry basket but only the top was there. I looked around for the bottoms and found them scrunched into a tight ball in the dustbin. I held them up to the light. There it was. Our £5,000 bloodstain.

When she returned two hours later I met her outside.

'Vic,' I began. Her orange tracksuit top was tied around her waist and a V of sweat had darkened her singlet underneath. Little wisps of hair stuck to her forehead and neck. 'Vic, I'm –'

'It's fine, Dan.' She looked at me, mouth agape, regaining her breath.

'It isn't fine. We should talk about this.'

She began marching on the spot, pumping her arms.

'I said it's fine.'

She gave me a smile I had never seen before. It was a receptionist's smile. A stranger's. It was chilling. She walked past me into the house and closed the door behind her. We didn't talk about it. Neither then, nor later. I didn't dare go near her. I kept picturing that smile.

That was the beginning of the exercise. She started getting up at five forty to run. A juice machine appeared and at six thirty every morning it would go off. The noise was terrible; like an angle grinder. Sometimes the sound would infiltrate my dreams and I'd picture her downstairs stuffing Alfred into it, filling the air with an explosion of green feathers and blood. We didn't have sex any more. That was over. She bought more orange clothes. A set of dumbbell weights appeared in the back room – Alfred's room. An aerobics step. She'd stand the iPad up and do whole routines. This went on for weeks. I felt she was becoming a stranger, that I was living alone. I felt less and less inclined to reach out, less capable.

'The forums say the healthier your body, the greater the chances of successful implantation. Seed and soil concept,' she said at six twenty-five one morning through a mouthful of raw carrot. 'In agriculture, fertile soil leads to greater yields. It's the same in the uterus.'

She joined a gym. She ran there from work, and after the gym she ran home. She insisted we charge our phones on the landing because the forums advised that LEDs and microwaves hindered recovery. She bought a sleeping mask and began piping birdsong into the bedroom through a gap in the door. In the half light of night I looked at her lying next to me, at her hands folded serenely over her chest. *Come back to me*, I'd say in my head, repeating the words over and over, *Come back to me*, hoping the words might somehow leap from my mind into hers. I started having dreams. Variations of the same dream. I was in a hall of mirrors and though I was alone I could immediately sense the panic of needing to locate Victoria and Ivy. I saw them and ran to them but it was never really them, it was their reflections, and I'd smash into a mirror. I turned and one of them would beckon me, gesturing with her hand but never speaking, and I'd run and again smash my face in.

Victoria arranged for a second round of IVF in May. One morning in March I caught a glimpse of her naked body. I had not seen it for a long time. It had changed so much. She was leaner, wiry. While she cleared a circle in the steamed-up mirror I climbed into the shower. It was such an odd situation; I felt estranged from her yet we conducted our daily lives with the same proximity as before. We were extras in a film. Things to do, but nothing to say. I closed my eyes and let the water pummel my face. I heard Victoria say something.

'What?' I yelled.

'I said I'm starting with my trainer tonight.'

'Oh. OK.'

The only ostensible difference the trainer made was that now Victoria came home later and more tired. She'd go straight into the kitchen to microwave one of the five identical dinners she'd pre-cooked at the weekend, put her earphones in and watch fitness videos on YouTube while she scooped the food into her mouth.

May came. Victoria was injected with more hormones. Then they sucked eggs from her body. Then they put one back inside her. After it was done, I guided her across the car park to the Transporter.

'Let's get you home.'

'I'm not coming home,' she said. 'I'm going to my

mother's. The forums all agree, every kilojoule you save after transfer increases the chances of successful implantation. My mother can look after me, bring me things.'

'You planned this? Why didn't you tell me? I could've done things for you. I could've looked after you.'

'You've got work,' she said feebly. She wouldn't look at me.

It would've been useless to protest. I dropped her at her parents' house and went straight to Jerusalem. When I arrived, Ivy wasn't in the bay window. I was told she was sleeping and was taken to her. The air was stale inside the tiny room. My mother was on her back, her head turned to the side on her pillow. I cracked open the window and looked out down the coast. The sea was crashing against the tide barriers and exploding high into the air like powder.

A few days went by with no contact from Victoria. On the fourth night as I lay awake in bed, I had what I now know was a panic attack. I was at a loss why. Was it stress? Was I lonely? Was this what loneliness feels like? I had to do something. So I did what anyone of my generation did when trying to solve a problem in their life: I googled it.

I typed I THINK I'M LONELY into the search bar and was presented with lists of suggestions, things I could do. For hours I sat in the glow of my old laptop, scouring these lists, searching for something. *Find a hobby. Buy a pet. Fall in love.* None of them were the answer, but I was on the Google merry-go-round, which, once you're on, is impossible to get off, and I kept searching into the wee hours, graduating to YouTube videos. And then finally, I found something.

In black-and-white, a man lies on his bunk inside a prison cell. He looks depressed. The music is sad. Cello, soft piano. A trolley is pushed along a corridor. Its wheels squeak. The prisoner becomes excited at the sound. The music becomes more hopeful. A hint of percussion. The prisoner stands up, his face now a picture of anticipation. There's a knock on the cell door and the hatch opens. Into the cell pours brilliant white light. The whole screen then fades to white. The sad cello is usurped by exultant strings and we see the prisoner, now in full colour, sat on his bed reading his letter. The voiceover says, 'Prisoners are people too. Become an Inbox Inmate today and change a person's life.' There was a warning: *Only begin writing to an inmate if you can commit. Abandoning your Inbox Inmate can have disastrous consequences for their mental wellbeing.* I clicked the link.

That night I dreamt I was in prison. Dark and silent with endless corridors of vacant cells. Victoria beckoned me to follow her and then turned and walked away from me. Each time I reached the cell into which she'd disappeared, she was gone. *Dan! Dan!* Victoria's voice called to me from somewhere unseen. *Dan! Dan!*

'Dan! It's half-ten! Why are you in bed?' Victoria was stood over me, shaking my body. I opened one eye. It took me a second to realise this was not part of the dream.

'You're back,' I said.

'Don't tell me you forgot?'

Half an hour later we were in the fertility specialist Dr Williams' office. He began asking Victoria a series of questions. He looked intently at his computer screen and clicked his mouse with every answer.

'Nausea?'

'No.' *Click.*

'Have you been to the toilet more?'

'No.' *Click.*

'Has there been any spotting?'

'No.' *Click.*

'And your period is due …?'

'Now. Today. And I'm like clockwork.' *Double click.* Then silence. He typed something. Victoria's leg bounced nervously. I wanted to reach out a hand, to touch her, calm her. But something stopped me.

'OK, I'm going to order some bloods.'

'You mean?'

***

Usually, when I'm writing I can block everything out. But this afternoon my attention was distracted by a buzzing sound outside. I stood on my chair to peer out of the window and scan the wide expanse of grass that comes right up to my window. I leant as far forward as I could, trying to look skyward. A circular black object, a tiny UFO, swooped out over the grass from directly above my window. Replete with rotors and antennae, the thing flew at speed towards the woods. It got so far and then slowly, in a controlled manoeuvre, set itself down. After a few moments it took flight again, rising straight up into the air, and flew off. I sat back at my desk and picked up my pen but my rhythm had gone. I can't force this thing. I mustn't. I can't write with a mixed-up head. All I could think of was the drone and the muggy heat in this room and the mirror frame Gordon has now asked me to make.

**

We were pregnant. And suddenly it was all Moses baskets, pushchairs, breast pads, stretch-mark lotion, expandable pants, nappies and body pillows. After Dr Williams told us the news there was a moment of stunned quiet, a sharp intake of breath, a deep reddening of her face, a single tear. But if Victoria felt any elation she had contained it. Like Superman swallowing a bomb. On the drive back to Beryl Avenue I caught her smiling. But there was no great reconciliation. No magical rebinding. I still couldn't touch her.

And yet I craved her love. But there was no formula for producing it. Her love was bestowed on you or it wasn't. Being with Victoria was like driving at night with no headlights. Occasionally, objects emerge from the dark and you steer away from them, you stay alive but you don't know where you're going. And if you stop to get out, where are you then? In the dark in the middle of God-knows-where. So your only option is to keep driving and hope the lights come on, all the while bracing yourself for a smash.

I built a rosewood cot and carved my name into one of the slats. I didn't tell Victoria about this. It would be my secret, my way of feeling closer to the baby. I made a chest of drawers with a little gulley on top for nappy changes. I made a rocking chair for nursing. I made a mobile from offcuts; trains, elephants, stars, the moon. I was trying.

One Saturday morning in July Victoria appeared in the workshop wielding two mugs of tea. I stopped working and looked at her. She was finally showing. In profile her belly was the shape of a teardrop of sap rolling down a tree. It finally hit me. I could see it. Touch it. Victoria offered me a mug. I stopped working and looked into her eyes and for the first time since this whole thing began, saw them looking back with warmth into mine. My hand went to her belly but stopped short of touching it. She grabbed it and pressed it onto the broad flank of the bump. It was taut and warm. We stood there for a while, not talking but occasionally looking up at each other and laughing.

Over the next few weeks, as we neared the end of the first trimester, things improved. We kissed one another goodnight again and occasionally reached out a hand to touch the other's arm. It was like we were a pair of nervous teenagers playing at being a real couple. Love recovers, it seemed. At least then.

July turned to August. One Tuesday night, while Victoria was at Yoganatal class, I moved all the new furniture into the nursery to surprise her. As I looked at the wooden slat with DANIEL carved into it, I realised the scope of my feelings had expanded now to encompass this other, this third. It had happened without my noticing. And it didn't feel as though my love had halved. It rather felt as though it had replicated and doubled, like cells dividing through mitosis.

Once all the furniture was in place I switched the light off and backed out of the nursery onto the landing. I heard a sound outside: an engine. Deep and thunderous and menacing. I went to the nursery window to look out onto the street. Victoria was approaching the house, her yoga mat under her arm. She was early. Then a black sports car – a souped-up coupé – rolled up alongside her. She waved to it. A friendly wave. A thank-you-for-the-ride wave. The coupé then screamed off down the street. Victoria was almost at the house now.

'You're back early,' I said descending the stairs. I followed her through to the kitchen. I decided not to ask about the coupé, I would give her the opportunity to bring it up herself. She retrieved one of her pre-prepared dinners from the fridge and put it in the microwave. Then she grabbed a plate and fork and filled a glass with water. She was saying nothing. If I wanted to know, I'd have to ask, she said silently. 'Did you get a lift?' I asked finally, I couldn't hold it back any longer.

'Yeah,' she said, too casually.

'From who?'

'Oh, just my PT. He was going this way anyway.' She downed half the water.

'You know if you don't want to walk home any more I can get you.'

'No, it's fine, I like the walk.'

'Just not tonight?'

'People are kind of insistent when you're pregnant. If you saw me get dropped off why are you even asking if I got a lift?'

'I didn't see you get dropped off. I saw you walking up the street and then wave to that car. At first I thought it was just someone you knew driving by. But since you told me you did get a lift I assume it was in that car?'

'Yes. What's going on here? I'm home ten seconds and you start grilling me?'

'So why did you get out halfway down Beryl Avenue?' I continued pushing. I could sense a lie. 'Why didn't you just get dropped off at the house?' *DING*. The microwave went off. She guided the steaming dish onto a tray and immediately filled her mouth with too-hot food, blowing to cool it even while she chewed. Buying herself some thinking time, I suspected.

'He says it's better to finish every journey on your own steam. Scott is really into wellness ...'

'Scott?'

'... he thinks of the body and the mind not simply as being connected to one another, but as one entity.' This she said with an ecstatic grin on her face. 'His sessions aren't just about physical strength. We meditate. Focus on mindfulness. He's very intuitive. He can sense when his clients are imbalanced. There's a WhatsApp group. He sends us inspirational quotes every morning.'

'Wait. He has your number?'

'He has all his clients' numbers. When he heard I was struggling to conceive – '

'You told your trainer about that?'

'I tell Scott everything. It's part of his philosophy. Clear mind, healthy body.'

This went on and on. With every word I grew more convinced of her delusion. I had begun to feel like she'd come back to me. But the truth was only her body had returned. Her mind remained out there, lost in some impenetrable pseudo-spiritual fog. We went to bed still talking about Scott's 'philosophy', about the women on the forums and their beliefs. As we lay there in the pitch darkness, birdsong in the air, we could've been two campers on the jungle floor. And as she explained the effects of 'pure cognitive energy' on the body, which involved 'willing your best self into being', I could think only of how surreal my life was and how great the distance between us had truly grown during those bleakest months. But the baby in her belly was mine. We were chained together now, for life. Whether or not she liked it.

I woke up in the middle of the night and was alone.

I got to my feet and left the bedroom. On the landing I heard a soft noise in the nursery. In all the Scott talk I'd forgotten the surprise I'd prepared for her. She must have woken in the night and found it herself. I approached the nursery door and knocked softly. She did not respond. I opened the door. She was sat in the rocking chair but did not turn to look at me as I entered. The light was off. I paused in the doorway, anxious not to encroach on what seemed a poignant moment, and simply watched. An image of my father doing this same thing came to me. He had built my first cot, my first bed, everything I owned. *Jesus was a carpenter*, Victoria had said to me all those years ago. Yes, as was his father, I thought now, and Jesus was his apprentice. It was Joseph who crafted the things of Jesus' life, not God, Joseph who had given him chairs to sit on and tables to eat at. Had my father found Ivy in the middle of the night like this too? Had Ivy sat in a chair he made and pretended to hold me in her arms, as Victoria did now? Had Ivy cried and cried with the sheer power of this new feeling expanding like a balloon inside her heart, as Victoria did now? I went to her. I wanted to touch her. I wanted to put my hand on her belly and feel the warmth of the blood pulsing through it. I wanted to feel the rhythm of her heart, and the jazz percussion of our baby's erratic movements. I looked down over her shoulder and saw that she was not pretending, that she held something in her hands. I whispered to her:

'What are you doing?' Incredible heat radiated from her. She was burning up. Her body shook violently beneath me as she suppressed convulsions. 'What's wrong?' I moved round to see her from the front. 'Vic?' I tried to soothe her, tried to get her to look at me but she would not look up from her lap. I followed her gaze.

I thought it was a doll. A doll made out of clay. Tenderly, she cradled it in her lap, which was soaked with blood. I knelt at her feet to look more closely at it, at the thing in her hands.

From the gravel path I can see my window. In the opposite direction lie the woods. The drone came down on the grass between the woods and my window. Sometimes I stare at the black wall of trees. I wonder: what's in there? What lies beyond the woods? I do it because I can't get the image of Victoria in the rocking chair out of my head. Sometimes at night I go to my window and focus all my cognitive energy on one spot at the wood's edge, a gap between two trees perhaps, and will *her* to emerge from them, to walk across the grass, place her palm on the reinforced window, smile.

Today on my walk I saw someone out on the grass. I have never seen anybody out there. I don't even know how to access it, it's blocked off by a tall fence. He was looking for something, with a long stick in his hand. It was hot and the man removed his hat and ran a tissue across his forehead. He started walking towards the path. When he saw me he waved.

'Dan the man!' he shouted. It was Gordon. 'How are you?'

'Fine. What're you looking for?'

'Oh, someone mentioned something about another drone. You never saw anything flying around yesterday by any chance?'

'Actually I did. It came down there,' I pointed roughly to where he'd been swiping his stick, 'and then flew off.'

'Which direction?'

'Woods.'

'You haven't seen anyone out there?'

'On the grass? Of course not.' Gordon looked towards the woods.

'How's that mirror frame coming along?'

***

It didn't hit me until weeks later that we'd lost a son. Conceived without us ever touching. An immaculate conception.

Victoria was never the same. The shock left her hollow, like the socket of a pulled tooth. Listening to Dr Williams' explanation-cum-theory of the reason for the miscarriage she did not react. She sat and played with her hands. And she did not share her grief with me. I barely saw her. I felt even my appearance was painful to her. When she came home she ate standing up in the kitchen then went straight to bed.

There is one photo of him. He is laid on a woolly blanket, swaddled in white cloth. His skin is red. His eyes are closed. His half-formed mouth is open as though in a stifled scream. He is about the size of an onion.

Inside the clinic's on-site chapel we were invited to name him by the female chaplain. Victoria refused. The chaplain turned to me. I could think of nothing. I said I was sorry. The chaplain said it was OK, God would name him. As we watched the tiny box move along the conveyor strip towards the open hatch, I felt my throat constricting. I squeezed but no tears would come. Victoria stood with her arms crossed. As the curtain came down I was suddenly seized by panic. I whispered my own name: 'Daniel'.

I wasn't about to leave the naming of my son to Him.

Victoria never spoke of him. I did however see that his photo had become the wallpaper for her iPad and her smartphone. Some nights, while I lay on the couch unable to sleep, I heard her crying in the bedroom above me.

As the sun set earlier and the afternoons became darker until eventually there was no afternoon, only morning and evening, Victoria's body went through another evolution. The goal before had been to create a healthy vessel: a body ripe for creation. Now, seemingly, the goal was to create a battering ram: a body capable of destruction. She was battling with everything. With her body, with the world, with God, even the seasons. As winter deepened, she made her appearance summery. She got spray-tanned and dyed her already blonde hair even lighter. She went running in the cold in crop tops and hot pants and when she got back her skin would be pink and numb.

One Sunday as I was leaving the house to visit my mother, Victoria suddenly appeared and slipped her jacket on. I watched her zip it up.

'Don't look so shocked,' she said.

When we got to Jerusalem, the car park was fuller than usual, as it was in the run-up to every Christmas. Inside, the nurse at the front desk signed us in.

'Where is she?' Victoria said. I pointed to my mother in the bay window, looking skyward. Victoria darted off in her direction. I grabbed her by the arm.

'Wait. She hasn't seen you for a long time. Let me go and tell her you're here and then I'll wave you over.' I walked around to the front of Ivy's chair and looked her in the eye. She smiled. Relief. Always relief when she recognised me. I kissed her head.

'Daniel,' she said.

'Hello Mum. I've brought someone to see you today.' I signalled to Victoria.

'Hello Ivy,' she said, kneeling before her.

'Victoria?' Ivy said. Victoria nodded and I could see she was beginning to cry. 'Victoria,' she said with more conviction. 'You're so thin.'

Victoria didn't respond to the comment. She began rummaging in her jacket pocket.

'I want to show you something,' she said. She produced a small square of glossy paper. It had been folded twice and she had to work it over repeatedly with the butt of her wrist to flatten it out. 'Look.' She placed it into Ivy's hands. Ivy held it up to her nose and squinted.

'That's your grandson.' Ivy looked up at me. Her eyes betrayed profound confusion.

'I have a grandson?'

'Yes Ivy. You have a grandson.' Ivy stared hard at the photograph of little Daniel's tiny swaddled body.

'He's beautiful,' she said. 'What's his name?' Silence fell upon us. We had never discussed names.

I cleared my throat. 'Daniel,' I said.

'Daniel,' Ivy repeated, 'of course.' Victoria looked sheepishly up at me and smiled as if to say *thank you*. 'So, where is he?' Ivy said, her eyes widening.

'He's sleeping,' said Victoria. This seemed to satisfy my mother and she went back to staring intently at the photograph. Perhaps in Victoria's mind this was her only chance to 'be' a mother, to pretend, even if just for an afternoon. Perhaps it was her gift to a dying old woman. Perhaps it was her way of exorcising pain.

'Does your father know he's a grandfather?' Ivy said, as though to confirm the cruelty of the world.

'No Mum. We haven't told him yet.'

'He'll be so happy. Can I keep this?' she said, pressing the photograph to her chest.

'Yes of course. It's for you,' Victoria said.

When we left Jerusalem I felt some kind of peace. Victoria looked like a person who had shed a great burden. She walked ahead of me to the Transporter. As in childhood I felt drawn to the seafront. I wanted to watch the retreat of the clouds. My mother and I used to yell at the sky after a storm had passed: *Go away clouds! You're not welcome!* In the north the outline of the Lake District's peaks began to show, and to the west the oil rig at the outer reaches of Wilder Bay. Victoria joined me, and we stood side by side in silence, just looking out.

Ivy died four days later, on Christmas Eve.

The funeral took place on New Year's Eve. Victoria didn't come. She went the night before to stay at her parents' house and sent me a text on the day saying:

I can't face it. sorry

I wasn't sure she'd ever come back. As the casket moved slowly, mechanically, towards the hatch, I pictured Daniel's sad little box. *It's OK*, the vicar had said, *God will name him.* Emotion came like a wave now and I was shaken by grief, deep and strong. The injustice was too great. Nobody else here knew about him. I was alone in my sadness. I kept turning around, hoping Victoria had changed her mind and slipped into the back of the church. I noticed a few of Frank's family had turned up. The sight of them made me sick.

Following the ceremony there was a buffet laid on at the cricket club.

Throughout the afternoon various people approached to shake my hand, to offer perfunctory condolences, and, more pertinently, to inform me they had to leave to get to their New Year's Eve parties and that they didn't want to hit traffic and so on. I didn't care. I wanted them gone. At one point Frank's sister, a crusty, overly made-up old woman, came over. She said she thought it was losing Frank that'd killed my mother, that she must've begun to die of a broken heart when he passed.

Once everyone had left I returned to the crematorium to collect the ashes. There was nobody there to greet me, but the outer door to the chapel was open and I went inside to find my mother's urn on a leaflet-covered table. There was a note from the vicar:

Daniel,

I had to leave to make my New Year's Eve engagements.

Please do take your mother's remains.

Yours with faith, love and best wishes for the New Year.

I placed the urn on the passenger seat and drove home. Though it was still early, parties were already in full swing. Fireworks going off, girls walking arm in arm through the windy streets clutching bottles of cheap prosecco.

Victoria used to keep a bottle of 'emergency' champagne under the kitchen sink so we'd be ready if ever there was cause for a sudden celebration. I poured myself a warm glass and shoved the bottle in the fridge. I hadn't eaten all day and the champagne went instantly to my head. Grimacing, I poured another glass and went through to the living room to watch telly.

A whole bottle of champagne later, bored and listless, I turned my laptop on. I went to my email inbox and saw an unread message at the top, with the subject

NEW YEAR'S EVE – It's not a party for everyone

It was from Inbox Inmate. *Dear Daniel*, it said, *tonight is a time for celebration, remembrance and looking to a brighter future. But for inmates, it can be a time of desperate loneliness and despair. Some may feel they have no future. Tonight, more than on any other night, they need you. Write to a prisoner now! You could save someone's life.*

How ironic, I thought, that I was being asked to save somebody's life, when I was sat here tallying up the ways in which my own had been destroyed.

Click here to send a message.

***

I have arrived at a critical juncture. I can't really go any further without a little commentary about the trial.

They took our letters. My letters to her and hers

to me. Both sides; the prosecution and defence both believing they'd find something within them that would shine the requisite light onto the dock. Character constructing. Or destructing. They took Victoria's iPad and smartphone and my old Nokia. But it was the letters we sent through Inbox Inmate that they really wanted, and that the press wanted (and somehow acquired).

Some of them were read aloud in court. The papers printed some choice lines but they didn't print the letters in their entirety. Like the prosecuting barrister, they needed a villain and a victim and it didn't serve their ends to provide the public with the whole story. *She* was the apple of the press's eye for a time. Beautiful and dangerous and with a tragic backstory.

If you've been mining the web for 'facts' you might have seen the letters yourself. I have copies of them all here. If the press hadn't got hold of them they would've been lost to me, behind a wall of legality. The Freedom of Information Act is a wonderful thing. But the thick black blocks of ink through the redacted places and names give the letters an air of secrecy and criminality that wasn't present before, when they were written. They were simply the missives of two damaged souls, reaching out for a connection.

***

Here is what I wrote that New Year's Eve:

Dear Prisoner,

Today I cremated my mother. She's been ill for a long time. Dementia. I have her remains here with me as I type. Ivy. That was her name.

    Vic didn't show up.

    I have no idea who I am writing to. Forgive me.

    I am suddenly very tired.

    Happy New Year.

Dan

I hit 'send' and fell asleep on the couch.

When I woke up, 2016 was six hours old, and my first act of the New Year was to run upstairs and dry-heave over the toilet.

In the living room my laptop was open on the floor. No more messages had arrived. There were no missed calls or texts on my Nokia. Nobody wanted to wish me a Happy New Year.

The next day I had an appointment with the solicitor about my mother's will. BAINBRIDGE & SON, the sign outside read, though the son had long since left Wilder and never returned. Bainbridge's 'office' was the converted garage of his semi-detached house. My father had done the conversion.

'This won't take long Daniel,' he began. 'Let's begin with your mother's financial assets.'

Bainbridge then informed me that my mother's

life savings – that is, the money she still had left from her inheritance from Frank (roughly thirty-six thousand pounds), who had been, besides an abuser and a domestic tyrant, a relatively successful property developer and landlord – was being donated to the Bowland Forest Shelter for Battered Wives. Bainbridge winced as he told me this, as though bracing himself for an angry reaction.

'Fine,' I said.

'OK then. Moving on to her physical assets.'

'What physical assets?'

'Your mother owned a small property, Daniel, in the country. Bequeathed by her late partner. You didn't know?'

***

Forgive me this interlude Lucy, but there is something bothering me and I can't concentrate.

I have this neighbour, Robbie. Robbie the Widower. He likes to come over to sit on my bed and watch my telly. He talks a lot. Asks a lot of questions. He comes over semi-regularly to sit and watch my telly. I barely watch the telly myself any more but I don't mind him watching it. He just likes to have some company and he isn't doing any harm. I just get on with my writing. The last time he came over he was very interested in your photograph. Who's the dish, he asked. I thumped him in the arm. His life hasn't gone the way he wanted it to either. He's hunched and scrawny and shrivelled up. But he is a sweet guy. And I like his company. But he does ask a hell of a lot of questions. What was I writing? I told him. Who's Lucy? I told him who you are. You're a dark horse, he said. Who's Ruby, he asked. I didn't answer that one. I moved the completed pages into the drawer. She your girlfriend? I closed my eyes and breathed and reminded myself that Robbie is lonely, that he is very lonely and this is just his way. Every visit of his ends with some sad comment about his departed wife. Today's was: My Maud used to have her secrets too.

The reason I'm bringing him up is that it has just struck me that I haven't seen him now in over a week, which is very odd. It didn't occur to me until I was down in the workshop this afternoon. It was the silence. After running the arris off a particularly sticky joint, I stepped back to admire my work and it suddenly hit me. I've got used to Robbie's presence. His company. I've come to value it as I thought he did mine.

Tomorrow I will seek out Gordon and ask him. If anyone is likely to know what's happened to Robbie it will be him. I hope he's all right.

***

So, I was finally a homeowner. I left Bainbridge's office

with the deeds to Frank's cottage. In the Transporter I read the address on the front page. There was no street name or suburb, just a postcode and a name: *Lanes End*. I put the documents back inside the envelope and drove home. When I put my key in the front door I knew instinctively that Victoria was back. I found her downing a glass of water at the kitchen sink. I put the keys and deeds down on the worktop. She was still dressing exclusively in orange. I wondered if this was simply through habit or whether she hadn't yet truly given up on having a baby.

'These are the keys to my mother's cottage. It's mine now. She left it to me in her will.'

'What? No way! Just like that?' She snatched the keys up and inspected them closely as if to verify that they were real. I nodded. A smile spread across her face as she picked up and began flicking excitedly through the deeds. 'What will you do with it?

On the drive back from Bainbridge's I had thought that I would sell it or rent it out, but seeing Victoria's happy reaction gave me an idea.

The next morning we drove to Lanes End. We drove through the centre of Wilder. Past key cutters, gold pawners and pound shops. We drove out past the empty marina, the lighthouse and the North Point Hotel, once visited, according to Wild' un lore, by Queen Victoria in 1900. We drove over the disused level crossing, out of the town and into farmland. Through lanes and lanes we drove and never once saw a single other vehicle. We got lost and turned back on ourselves numerous times and eventually – using Victoria's intermittent 4G signal – we identified the entrance to the property.

The cottage itself sat at the far end of a large grassy clearing surrounded on three sides by dense dark woods. To the right of the cottage were a couple of outbuildings. I parked the Transporter in a shale-covered space, a courtyard of sorts, between the outbuildings and the cottage. There was a large shed at the farthest end of the clearing.

We went in the cottage's side door. It was dim and cool. An old wax jacket hung from a peg on the wall. I reached what appeared to be the centre of the cottage: the point at which two corridors crossed. A half-open door beckoned me into a large bedroom. I walked to its bay window, which overlooked the clearing out front, and listened. It was so quiet.

There was a sitting room with a hearth, and a kitchen in which I found the half-rotted, blackened corpse of a mouse, stuck fast to the floor, and some letters addressed to a Ms Constance Lovett. She must've been the tenant Mr Bainbridge told me about, who had died here alone, the last of her family. Holding her unopened mail in my hands I wondered how she'd died. Where. The shelves were bare except for a single plate commemorating the wedding of Charles and Diana. There was no power. It must've been cut ages ago. 'Imagine living in this little dark place by yourself,' Victoria said, wandering in. She went to take the plate down from the shelf but fumbled it to the floor. Bits of it went everywhere. 'Shit!' she hissed. I found a shovel leaning against a corner and used it to scoop up the fragments of Charles's broken face and the mouse's body and threw them into a dustbin outside the back door. Outside I took a few crunching steps across the shale towards the pines. I could hear the sea. When I returned to the kitchen I saw that the mouse had left a stain on the red tile; an imprint of its bones. I scraped at it with my boot but it seemed indelible. It would require chemicals.

Victoria had disappeared. I called to her and followed her voice to a tiny bedroom. 'Look at all this stuff,' she said as I entered, indicating the stack of plastic storage cartons in the corner. I pushed the door open wider, flooding the room with dim grey light. One of the cartons lay open on the bare single bed beside her. 'It's someone's old things. It's creepy. And there's no power. And there's dust and leaves everywhere.' I left her and entered the only room I hadn't been in yet. Though it was identical in dimensions to the box room adjoining it, it felt bigger thanks to a large south-facing window. I walked across the room and pressed my forehead to the glass.

'Oh,' I heard Victoria say behind me. I turned and saw her standing in the doorway, a hand raised to her mouth. I followed her gaze to the back corner of the room, to a wooden swinging cot. She walked to it and touched it. The cot swung stiffly on its hinge.

'You really see us living here,' she asked.

'I'll do it up.'

'There's barely any furniture.'

'I'll make furniture. And I'll fix the electrics and the water and everything else. Vic,' I said, moving closer to the cot, 'I really think this place could be our fresh start.'

'I don't know, Dan.'

'I thought if we moved here, maybe we could try again.' I let this hang in the air between us. She placed both her hands on the rim of the cot and stared down into it.

Beryl Avenue was draining the life from us. But I had a mission now: I would make Lanes End into a home and get us out of that place. I felt invigorated, giddied by a new sense of purpose. I saw weeks and weeks laid out before me. It was a race against time, against the sinking of the ship. I would have to work all the hours available to me.

When we arrived back at Beryl Avenue, Victoria paused with a hand on her seatbelt buckle. She seemed about to say something to me but then changed her mind and went inside. Dressed all in orange, she disappeared into the dark hallway like a lantern into the night sky.

That evening while Victoria was at Battle Ropes class, I received an email from Inbox Inmate. It took me right back to New Year's Eve. How petulant and foolish I'd been to write anything at all that night. Mortified – and curious – I opened it. What crazy, tattooed convict had responded to me? How would he react to the drunken missive I'd fired off after my mother's funeral? I scanned the message top to bottom and noticed something strange. A woman's name? Surely, that must be a mistake.

Ruby.

Reading her name for the first time I felt, as you feel fine dust settle on your arm if you sit very still, a tiny speck of danger attach itself to my life.

***

Lucy, forgive me.

A little over a month ago you so kindly wrote to me and have had nothing by means of reply from me since. I could not blame you for wondering if everything you've heard about me were true after all. I daresay you've had to endure a few I told you so's.

At times over the past month it has felt like you

were here in this little room with me. This sensation has made it so much easier for me to set things down on paper; to imagine I am not writing these words for you to read (or ignore) in the future but that I am simply speaking them to you.

I've been at such pains to paint you the fullest picture possible that I lost my grip on time. I realised, as I wrote her name just now, with a right hand that aches and closes in on itself like a claw, that to continue writing this as one letter would only lengthen my silence. I feel myself rushing these sentences. But Ruby is not a topic I can rush. So I've decided to drop the curtain here and insert an intermission.

Please don't feel the need to respond to this first letter, though of course I should be very glad if you did. It's late now, I will sleep and begin again in the morning.

Affectionately yours,

D

2

RUBY

September 2033

Dear Lucy,

I'm sick.

Three nights ago I went to sleep thinking happily of waking and picking up where I left off, picturing a full and peaceful morning's writing here at my desk with the sun shining down on your photo. But I awoke with a woozy head and haven't written a word since. When I place my foot on the ground I feel like I am trying to step from a moving train.

Your half-finished gift lies untouched down in the workshop. But this pencil in my hand feels like a crowbar; I can't imagine lifting an actual tool in my current state.

It is now the third day of September and I haven't spoken to another person for nearly two weeks.

Yesterday I was completely wiped out. I felt hot then cold then hot and I had a muddled brain and I couldn't focus on anything without feeling a terrible strain at the back of my head. I spent the day sleeping or half-sleeping and nibbling dry crackers under my sheet. In the middle of the night (or was it day?) I thought I heard a sound outside my window. Rustling, like something moving through the grass. I hauled myself to the window to investigate. I couldn't see anything out there. But once my eyes adjusted, the black trees caught my attention. Propped against the wall I watched them gently sway. To my mind, which had begun to play tricks on itself, it was like a giant wave *hello*. A smaller black thing, a figure, entered my field of vision, scurrying and skulking like an animal, fast, towards the trees. But it wasn't an animal, it moved on two legs. I tried to focus on it but my head stung and I had to squint and then turn away as a cold wave of nausea washed over my body. When I looked again, the figure was gone.

I am writing this after a very strange visit from Gordon. He called this afternoon out of the blue. I let him in, sat down on the bed – which is where I have lived now for four days – and offered him the chair. Straight away I could tell something wasn't right with him. He was oddly stiff. He made me nervous. I fidgeted with the bed sheets, started pulling them around me. *Can't Cook,*

Won't Cook was on the telly. I switched it off. The chef's strident laughter was hell.

'Is everything all right?' I asked. Gordon sat at my desk slowly, wearily. Still he did not speak. He looked for a moment at your photo and then opened the desk drawer. I hadn't the strength to protest.

'What's this?' he produced the pages I managed to get down a couple of days ago. 'A letter?' I nodded. 'Lucy eh?' he said and then looked up at your photo. He laughed. 'Good for you Danny. I haven't seen you out on your walks recently. You're normally so consistent. I can tell what time it is from where you are along the path. I was thinking, as I was tucking into my roast beef last night and looking across the table at my wife, I haven't seen Danny for a while. I'll call on him tomorrow.'

'I've been unwell. Virus, I think. I'm over the worst of it now.'

'I see.'

'I've been in bed for four days.'

'You need a wife, Danny.'

'Yes.'

He turned at one point and stuffed his fingers into the video-cassette slot in the telly. He rummaged around in there for a few seconds then inspected the dust on his fingers.

'Do you want a cup of tea or anything?' I offered, to break the silence more than anything.

'Some concerns have been raised,' he said, leaning forward conspiratorially.

'What concerns?'

'Over unsavoury behaviour.'

'Unsavoury?'

'Yes. In the woods.'

'Oh.'

'You have a view of everything from here. Have you noticed anything out of the ordinary?'

I thought of the black figure rushing across the grass towards the treeline last night. But as the words bubbled to the surface, it suddenly seemed foolish to mention it. I couldn't be sure I hadn't imagined it. I shook my head.

'I'm looking into it, trying to put people's minds at ease. So if you do happen to see anything out there, let me know.' He rose to his feet.

'Have you seen Robbie lately?' I asked as he reached the door. 'I haven't seen him for a couple of weeks. I knock but there's never any response. I haven't checked for a few days because I've been ill.'

He put his hat back on and looked at me blankly. 'I hope you're feeling better soon Danny,' he said. Then he left.

**

This is Ruby's first letter to me:

1 January 2016

Hello Dan,

First things first. Happy New Year! I know it's not exactly been a happy start to the year for you but it feels weird not to say it on January 1.

I'm so sorry to hear about your mother. Ivy is such a great name. I love ivy. If the world ended ivy would take over.

Do you believe in God? I never used to, but lately I've started to wonder. There's so much badness, it can't all be coincidence. Did you know there is a type of flea that is perfectly designed to burrow into your heel and then feed on your blood and expand up to 2,000 times its size inside your foot?

No one has ever written a letter like yours before. People write to me because I'm in prison but they don't know what to say to me because I'm in prison. It's the elephant in the cell. I get so many of the same letter. I can feel their unease. They're writing on eggshells. Some are like news bulletins updating me on current events in the world. I've been having a yearlong conversation with an elderly man about politics. He doesn't realise we have TVs here. I humour him. How many people would take the time to hand-write letters to a person they've never met? He must be very lonely. Perhaps he's a widower? I can sense the questions he really wants to ask me bubbling beneath the surface. But he never does.

People write to me about 'safe' things. The letters are like press releases. Everything in them is perfect and sweet. Which is nice, but I read the words and I feel like I'm having a conversation with someone through a car window.

Your letter was different. It was raw. I could sense your pain. I couldn't wait to write back to you. Reading it I felt like Julia meeting Winston for the first time! (Have you read *Nineteen Eighty-Four*? Sorry, if you haven't you won't get the reference. If not, you must!) I want to know more about you. I want to hear about Ivy and this mysterious 'Vic'. Don't worry, I'm not some weirdo who leeches off the pain of others. I just like to listen and help people where I can. My twin says that's my fatal flaw. You're a fixer, she says. I prefer to say that I'm just addicted to people. My sister is so sweet. Of course she's right; I do love to fix problems. Or try to. I was an art psychotherapist before. In here I'm a Listener, with a capital L. I volunteer for the Samaritans. I *woman* the phones, listen to people. Do my bit. Most of the other volunteers do it for a change of scenery, for some time away from their cell. I do it because I love to help people. The trouble is, every time you 'listen' you get new people. You never get to speak to the same person twice. There's no way of reconnecting.

Once the caller goes, another one comes through and you don't know if what you've said has helped. I like to believe that it does. Kind words always help.

When I read your letter I sensed a person reaching out. I got the impression that the words you typed came from an honest desire to connect.

I used to get people to paint and draw their feelings. I used art as a sort of distraction therapy. Just paint what you feel, I'd say. And out would come these amazing pictures – sometimes abstract, other times perfectly legible – like scans of the contents of their souls. And it was a starting point; we'd analyse their work together and they'd begin to describe what they'd done and they didn't realise they were in therapy any more. It was like crushing and hiding a pill in the dog's dinner.

I hope you write back. You'll be surprised at how much it helps to just get stuff down on paper. So, Dan, just write what you feel.

Ruby

I didn't intend to write back to her. But of course I did.

Our tenancy at Beryl Avenue would expire at the end of June. I had just under six months to whip Lanes End into shape.

The day I rewired the cottage and reconnected the

electricity felt like a major milestone. Restored to light and power, the cottage seemed to offer a glimpse of a life. I discovered a trove of antique furniture inside the smaller of the outbuildings. Chests, chairs, tables, wardrobes, a grandfather clock, even a Chinese folding screen, all tucked away under dustsheets. There was enough furniture to fill the entire cottage. Buoyed by the discovery, I drove home quickly.

A black coupé was parked outside the house. I pulled onto the drive and approached the car. The coupé's engine fired into life. I knocked on the tinted window and it lowered with an electronic wheeze.

'Scott, is it?' I thrust my hand through the open window towards him. He gripped it limply. I could feel thick callouses on the palm of his hand. 'You're Vic's personal trainer right?' The coupé growled and hummed. 'What are you doing here?'

'He's here to pick me up,' Vic's voice came from behind me. She was wearing a tracksuit top and yoga pants and had her gym bag slung over her shoulder.

'What time is it?' I said.

'Six.'

'You don't normally go to the gym this early in the evening.'

'Class times all changed in January.' She walked around the front of the coupé and threw her bag onto the back seat. 'You've been at the cottage so much lately you mustn't have noticed,' she said, across the roof of the car. She got in.

'What time will you be back?' I said, bending down to Scott's window again. She looked at Scott, then at me, and said:

'Around eight thirty.' This sounded like a question.

'Right.' Scott pushed a button on his steering wheel and a thumping dance track erupted from the car like thunder.

'Turn that down!' Victoria barked at him. There was a tone of familiarity in her voice that I disliked very much.

'Well, have a good workout or whatever. It was good to meet you,' I said, these last words drowned out completely by a couple of monstrous engine revs. Scott's side window rose and the coupé sped off.

I watched the empty street for a while and listened to the coupé's engine recede farther and farther away. I went inside, fed Alfred and sat at the dining table with my laptop. As the old machine whirred into life I began already composing the opening lines of my first proper letter to Ruby.

Here is what I wrote:

16 January 2016

Dear Ruby,

I am so embarrassed by what I wrote on New Year's Eve. I wasn't myself that night. I could not have expected such an understanding response.

It feels nice to be writing to a Listener. I feel like I haven't been listened to for a long time. Vic hears me but she doesn't listen. The 'mysterious' Vic is my partner by the way. We've been together just over five years. These days I can't figure her out. She's maddening and evasive. She did not come to my mother's funeral, that is true, but she had her reasons. I can't believe I'm opening up like this to a stranger!

As it happens I have read *Nineteen Eighty-Four* and I understood your reference. My father was big into books. He was a carpenter, like me, but his great passion was reading and he encouraged me to read as much as possible growing up. He used to say the only reason he became a carpenter was so he could make himself a nice reading chair. *Don't be like me*, he'd say. He was referring to his profession of course, he didn't want me to work with my hands. But he was such a peaceful soul, so calm, so in control of everything, so content. There was always this serene almost enlightened smile on his face, as though he was privy to some secret of the universe nobody else was. As though what he knew removed any worldly concerns from his head. How could I not have wanted to be like him? He died when I was twelve. I used to read all the time. I used to lie on the rug at his feet and read 'serious' books to try and impress him. I haven't read a single page of a book since he died.

My mother left a cottage to me in her will. I'm renovating it. I want to move there with Vic and start over. I finally got the lights to work today, which sounds insignificant now that I've typed it, but it felt like a big deal. I wanted to tell Vic but she dashed off as soon as I got home so I'm telling you about it instead.

Please, Ruby, tell me about *you* too. Where were you born? Where did you grow up? Is your twin identical?

Sorry, there's no order to this letter. I am writing these thoughts as they pop into my head. Are you analysing me as you read? Am I being selfish writing to you like this? I feel I should be asking about you, not burdening you with my problems. But you're right, it is cathartic to get stuff down. It's only taken me twenty minutes to write this letter, I haven't stopped typing. It has come pouring out of me like water from a tap.

Can I trust you? Are you real?

Dan

I wasn't entirely sure what I had begun, and with whom, but I was so lost and so alone that there seemed nothing to lose in seeing it through.

You've been at the cottage so much lately. Vic's words came back to me. The implication, that *I* was the one who had pulled away, the injustice of this, made me burn with anger. What were a few harmless letters in the face of her infidelity (I was sure of it now)?

It was nine o'clock when Vic came home. I was in the workshop. She looked at me from the bottom of the driveway. Our eyes met. She pretended she hadn't seen me and went inside. I heard Scott's coupé drive off.

That night I dreamt about Jerusalem. It was empty apart from a single person sat in the bay window. Down on the beach my mother was leaning backwards into the wind. I watched her for a while, like I was the parent. Behind me the person sitting in my mother's chair spoke. It was Victoria. She wore a white nightgown, bloodied between her thighs. Oscar was in her lap, his little wings flapping frantically. There were green feathers at her feet. She stared out of the window, an oddly intense look of concentration on her face. It dawned on me that she was throttling the bird. Suddenly, just when it seemed he was about to stop struggling, she released him and he flew away. *You saw that, right?* she said. *Tell me you saw that?*

A couple of days later I got this reply from Ruby:

23 January 2016

Dear Dan,

You can trust me. I am real.

I understand why you ask. I'm not offended. It's hard knowing who to trust. You can spend a lifetime with a person and not really know them. I don't blame you for questioning me. After all, who am I? Just a name on your computer screen.

I've needed something like this. A true exchange. You've come along at just the right moment. I promise never to judge you for anything you share with me. Will you promise the same?

Your father sounded like a wonderful man. It must have hit you very hard when he died. My sister Jade (yes, we're identical) and I never really knew our father growing up. He left our mother and moved to Spain with his girlfriend when we were two. Once every couple of years he'd fly us over to his villa. We'd play in the pool all day or go to the market with his maid. And after a few weeks of that he'd drive us to the airport in his convertible and check us in with the chaperone service and wave us off. *My two precious stones*, he called us.

How is Vic maddening? People talk about the

'seven-year itch' in relationships but it can occur at any moment. You've been together for over half a decade. It's reasonable to have some doubts. Or have I completely got the wrong end of the stick here? If it would help to talk about this then do. I'm not trying to analyse you.

Seeing as you asked so nicely, here is a bit about me: I practised art-psych in sunny Stoke-on-Trent, where I grew up. I wanted to be a painter but had no real talent so I spoke to a careers adviser who told me I should look into being an art therapist. That or retail. So I applied for the course and after four years I was a fully fledged psych with my own little NHS clinic in Stoke. And I loved it!

My problem was becoming too attached to patients. If they didn't show for a session I'd become frantic. I'd call all the numbers in their file. I'd visit them at home. I'd want to know why. I needed to know why. That was easily the hardest part of the job. In order to do my job well I had to care. But then how do you switch it off? How do you let someone leave your clinic and go back to what you know is an awful home situation and just move on to the next patient? I struggled with that problem for the whole time that I practised.

I suppose that's what did for me in the end. I met Lee through the clinic.

Changing the subject: did you grow up in your mother's cottage? I bet it's hard being there, seeing her things and smelling her smells? Describe it to me. I'm picturing stone walls and daisies, grass, trees, birds.

Ruby

This letter was breezy – like her first – but in this one I sensed something, a darkness, behind her words. She said she had problems detaching herself from patients. Had something in her own life made her that way? Certainly, it seemed her relationship with her father was a source of pain.

And who was Lee?

I realised, when I finished reading her letter, that I had been shaking the entire time. Was I afraid? Or was I excited?

January ended, giving rise to the annually occurring false hope that the worst of winter was over. Of course, the season found a way to deepen, as it does every February. I decided to wait a while until I wrote again to Ruby.

In the process of moving the antiques from the smaller outbuilding into the cottage – including an ornate and unfortunately defunct old grandfather clock – I discovered that the outbuilding would make a perfectly sized workshop.

Despite being filled now with furniture, the cottage still felt desolate. There was something unnerving about its atmosphere. Each day, in the moments between packing up my tools and walking across the shale to the Transporter, I would stand where the criss-crossing corridors met and listen. Old houses talk when you listen, my father used to say. But Lanes End didn't. The only sounds came from outside: the rustling of the pines and the distant crashing of waves.

One night in early February I came home from Lanes End to a surreal situation. The door to the back room – Alfred's room – was closed, which it never was, and I could hear an unfamiliar voice on the other side. I could just about make out the words *Hi, I'm Vicky*, then a pause, then *Hi, I'm Vicky* again with a slight change in cadence. I opened the door and went in. Victoria screamed. She was clad fully in exercise gear. A yoga mat had been rolled out on the floor. There was a tripod on the dining table and a digital camera was screwed in place on top. The room resembled a film set, with a pair of spotlights rigged up on boom stands pointing at her from the corners of the room.

'What are you doing?' I said. She began fighting with the camera, which emitted a series of double bleeps that ascended and then descended in pitch.

'Fucking thing. Stop recording!'

'Sorry. What exactly did I interrupt?'

'Nothing.'

'What is all this stuff?'

'What does it look like? It's Scott's vlogging rig,' she said, looking closely at the camera and mashing its many buttons.

'I thought Scott was a personal trainer.'

'For crying out …' She put the camera down on the dining table and held the back of her hand to her forehead. She closed her eyes and took a few slow deep breaths. Then she said, in a voice stripped of anger, 'Scott is not just a PT. He is a wellness coach. He also happens to be a vlogger.'

'Why do you have it?'

'Scott wants to reach out to as many people as possible. He's expanding his channel and has asked me to get involved. He wants to empower women.'

'His channel?'

'His YouTube channel.'

'I had no idea he had a YouTube channel.'

'Why would you? You never ask about my life, about any of this.' She threw a hand in the air to indicate that she meant everything. We fell silent.

'What's his channel's name?' I asked after a while.

'*Live Well With Scott* … You think it's stupid?'

'How does he empower women exactly?'

'Dan, if you're just going to …'

'… I want to know. I'm interested.'

She looked at me sceptically and then said, 'Wellness is just as much about the mind and soul as it is the body. That's his core principle. He wants to touch as many people as possible. An important part of his vision is the inclusion and empowerment of women. He wants to get more women watching his channel and taking an interest in their spiritual *and* physical fitness. He asked me if I'd be interested in getting involved and I said yes.'

'So you'll be making videos of yourself doing yoga?'

'To start with. And then maybe nutrition advice and meditation techniques as well as some gym-based work-outs for women.'

'I remember when I couldn't even get you to walk to the shops with me.'

'Yes, well,' she coughed dryly, 'that was a long time ago. Scott has a real sense of mission,' she added sombrely, addressing her feet.

'Would you like to come see the cottage soon?' I surprised myself by asking. As I heard myself saying these words, tears began inexplicably to form in my eyes. I looked to the ground so she would not see.

'Maybe,' she half-whispered.

So much invisible weight hung in the air between us. I felt it, this weight, pushing me down, pinning me in place, crushing me. Did she? Knowing now how she acted that October, I feel certain that she must have. But then, looking down and being mesmerised by the complex and baffling patterns on her orange trainers, and being unable to open my mouth to say ... what exactly? ... I felt alone in my despair. The heat from the spotlights was unbearable and I began to sweat. Victoria stood before me serenely. Ruby had asked me how Victoria was maddening; this was how! I wanted to scream, to rip and tear at her flesh and drag out the real Victoria, my Victoria, who was trapped inside.

'When will I be able to watch you?' I said, miserably.

'I don't know. Scott says I should practise until I'm comfortable in front of the camera first.'

'I see. Well, I'll leave you to it then. Do you want the door shutting?'

'Please.'

I went into the kitchen and stood at the sink. I looked at my reflection in the black window. Like my mother in Jerusalem, I was diminished, distorted and blurred, half filled in with darkness. I heard Victoria's suddenly loud and happy voice from the back room. *Hi, I'm Vicky ...*

Later that evening I wrote again to Ruby. There's no need for me to describe how I felt writing it. It is better simply to copy it out below:

3 February 2016

Dear Ruby

I'm fairly certain Vic's having an affair with her personal trainer.

I met him recently. He is a cartoon character. All muscle and hair. She sits there texting him night and day and thinks I don't notice. Well I do, and I am a fool and a coward for not saying anything. I think she knows that I know. And I think she knows that I will say nothing, will do nothing.

How did we get here? We tried for years for a baby but couldn't conceive. The failure hardened her. Then, through IVF, we finally conceived but she miscarried at thirteen weeks. Too young for a birth certificate.

There was time before the miscarriage and there is time after. We stopped trying.

And now there is Scott. I don't know what to do. What if she loves him? What if he has found a way to insinuate himself into her life?

And now I have this cottage. Building us a new home, making a place for us to begin again is all I feel I can do now. I fear that if I confronted her about Scott, I would be handing her something with which to twist and wrench free the last nail holding us together.

I want to leave this place, this ghost house. I want to tear it down. I want to destroy it. I want to destroy him.

Writing this letter has not made me feel better, as I hoped it would. But it has at least aired the wound, allowed me to look down and see what I'm dealing with.

Dan

I spent the following days wandering around in a stupor. I didn't want to think about *him*, them together, or anything. But I found myself looking at her, watching her texting him (undoubtedly him!) and smiling that smile which used to be shown only to me. I was tired and irritable all the time. I told myself it was stress, cumulative fatigue. Every night when I went up early to bed she'd say 'I'll be up soon,' but I could never stay awake long enough to feel her lying down beside me. And every morning when I awoke she'd already be up and gone.

I continued working on Lanes End. By the time I finished the kitchen, most of February had passed. Ruby still had not replied to my last letter. One evening I sat at the kitchen table and wondered: have I said too much? Had I scared her off? I felt my face blaze with shame and embarrassment. Had I been abandoned now by a convict, as well as my girlfriend?

As I looked up and watched the bare light bulb swing in the draught, which seemed impossible to eradicate, I had a premonition that I was destined to inhabit this place by myself, that it would become a tomb.

I'm almost better now. Today I felt strong enough to go outside. Happily, I haven't completely missed summer. The light is still soft, the air warm. I couldn't wait to get out there and feel the sun on my skin. It was so beautiful, I was surprised not to encounter anyone else on the path. But I did see a man in a baseball cap shambling around, hands in his pockets, head bowed. I recognised his hunched gait. Was it …? I began to trail him. At one point he stopped and turned around. I had been sure it was Robbie but when I saw his face I didn't recognise it. The features were wrong. He began talking to a small group of people congregated in the shade of a wall, people I did not recognise or know Robbie to have an association with. He did not take his hands from his pockets as he spoke, and when their brief interview was over he continued on along the edge of the gravel and around a corner. I followed him but when I rounded the corner he was gone.

At around quarter to two the sun darted behind a cloud and I felt a droplet of rain on my nose. Before I returned inside I called on Robbie but he did not answer. I have written him a note (copied below), which I will slip under his door tomorrow.

Robbie

I haven't seen you for nearly a month. I'm worried.

Have you seen Gordon lately? He's acting weird. Call soon.

D

If he doesn't come over after that, I will have no choice but to report it.

* * *

After some more fretful but productive days I finally received a response from Ruby. I took my laptop up to bed to read it while Victoria sat playing on her smartphone in the lounge.

Here is what she wrote:

22 February 2016

Dear Dan

I cannot even begin to imagine what losing a child feels like. I had patients who lost children. But I never really knew what to say to them. Their problem seemed so much bigger than my experience. I felt totally unequipped to help them. All I can say to you is that I am so terribly sorry.

Regarding this Scott person, sometimes people just do things and they couldn't tell you why if you asked them because they haven't even stopped for a second to ask themselves the same question. Sometimes people just act. No thought, just action. Especially when they've been through something awful they become sensory creatures, operating purely on the basis of what feels good or least bad.

You spoke of anger in your letter. Be careful, Dan. If you let anger build up inside you it will find a way to come out by itself. Trust me on that. Jade says that I absorb the feelings of others, that I'm like a jar of water a painter uses to wash his brushes. In my line of work I was exposed to so many extreme situations. I had to listen and not react. I cried sometimes, in the toilets while they were drawing or painting. It was like opening a valve, releasing the pressure. I felt I could have cried for days. I controlled everything pretty well for a time. But when I met Lee everything changed.

Lee was a patient. We became lovers. Ethically it was wrong, morally it was wrong. Plus, yes, stupid. Nuclear stupid.

Lee was quiet during our sessions. A big guy but softly spoken. As a child he was beaten regularly by his father. He'd seen his mother beaten half to death and spent three months in care while she recovered. He asked me out after our last session together. To begin with I said no but there was this attraction I couldn't overcome. One evening about a month after he left my care he turned up outside my clinic. He asked me out again. I couldn't help myself. We went to a bar and that night I slept with him. For a long time it was great. But I could tell he was acting. He was conscious of his issues – anger, general anxiety disorder, panic attacks, we'd discussed them in the clinic – but when we were together he hid them.

We moved in together. Things began OK. But then he started being cold towards me, snapping at me over little things. And then he started to hurt me. He'd grab my arm a little too firmly or shove me aside with his shoulder. He hit me once – out of nowhere, over a squabble – and then immediately fell into torrents of tears and begged for forgiveness. He didn't hit me for ages after that. But he devised another, far more insidious way to hurt me. Piece by piece, he arranged everything in our lives so that every move I made resulted in my own defeat. Let me explain.

First, he began announcing the time when I arrived home. 'Six forty.' 'Six thirty-nine.' 'Six forty-one,' when I came through the door. If I got home even just one minute later than he expected he'd be displeased for the rest of the evening and I'd be fighting to win back his approval. He used this to get me to have sex with him every night. I was too afraid to disappoint him again, so I just went along with it.

My work suffered. I zoned out thinking about which route to take home. I found myself rushing the last couple of patients so I could get away sooner. The odd time I had a cancellation in the last session I'd race home and park around the corner until it was the 'correct' time for me to arrive home. Then he put all the household bills in my name. He didn't like being left alone, so if I ever went to visit Jade or a friend he'd say 'you've got one hour' and for every minute I was late he threatened to run up all the bills until I got home; he'd call expensive numbers, turn on all the appliances, stuff like that. So I started cutting short my social engagements to make sure I was home on time. Inevitably, I stopped seeing people altogether. He made me sell my car and started ferrying me to and from work himself. Without my car I was cut off, completely isolated. Now I relied on Lee for everything. He convinced me to let him have control of my money. He made me add his name to my bank account. He didn't work. When I got paid he transferred the money into another account, his own I suppose, and then he'd pay me a weekly allowance of £50. This was for everything. My personal hygiene began to suffer. And I was so tired. He had me up until one or two in the morning having sex. It always hurt. I started fantasising about buying soothing gel for my vagina that could take the burn away. But I couldn't afford anything like this. So I sat on bags of ice wrapped in paper towels. One day the bag burst. I was too ashamed of the real reason my trousers were damp so I told my manager I had 'had an accident'.

He rarely hit me, and he was savvy enough never to touch my face. He'd jab me in the base of my spine or in the stomach. He broke my right big toe once under the heel of his boot. I couldn't walk without pain for weeks. This violence only ever happened about once or twice a year. But it was enough to keep me in line.

This went on for about two years. One day a patient asked if I was OK. She'd suffered similar abuse herself and I could tell she recognised the signs. I burst into tears. I couldn't stop. I was hysterical, struggling to breathe. She comforted me. She understood. He's controlling you, she said. You have to leave him. I knew then, as I was crying in front of her in my office, that it was over. The next day I called Jade from the office and asked her to meet me. As soon as I saw her I cried. I managed only to say the word 'Lee' and she intuited the rest. She said she knew some guys who could hurt him. When she left me that day she simply said: sit tight.

That night during dinner the doorbell went. Lee looked at me across the table. He put a finger to his lips. The doorbell rang again. He dropped his fork onto his plate and went to open the door. I saw two men in baseball caps. Lee tried to slam the door shut but one of them shoved his arm through. In the struggle I ran upstairs and out of sight. My phone rang. It was Jade. She told me to get out now. I heard the front door slam and the chain lock go on. Then I heard footsteps pounding up the stairs. Oh my god he's coming, I said and hung up. I was on the landing. When he was almost at the top of the stairs he reached up and yanked my ankle from beneath me. I fell backwards onto the landing, stunned and winded. He climbed on top of me and began punching me in the stomach and ribs. I kicked and struggled and managed somehow to rise to my knees. He wrapped his arm around my waist and started to pull me down again. I grabbed the banister. He was trying to pull me free so he could throw me down the stairs but he lost his grip and fell backwards himself. I turned to look down. The thick wooden post at the bottom of the stairs had been snapped like a cocktail stick. His legs were bent completely back at the hips. His feet touched the floor either side of his head. His right arm was underneath his body. His left arm was out by his side but facing the wrong way. I heard then the sound of the door being kicked. It burst open and the two guys in baseball caps came in, their fists primed. But they took one look at Lee's broken body and ran off.

Jade waited with me for an ambulance to arrive. They took me to hospital and treated my injuries, which were many but not serious. The next day a female police officer interviewed me from my hospital bed. I told her everything. I should've held my tongue. But I thought I was the victim. I thought I was just giving a statement, helping them sew this thing up. I'd suffered Lee's supremacy for years; it didn't even occur to me that I might be in trouble.

The next morning I was arrested and charged with attempted murder. I was facing a sentence of twenty-four years.

The prosecution accused me of plotting to kill Lee. Jade had put the idea in my head, they said, and we had been scheming for weeks. The kicked-in door, the fact that the two guys had ran off both proved this, they said. They used our relationship with our father as 'evidence' we hated men. Lee testified that I'd pursued him romantically when he was my patient, that I manipulated him into being with me. He made out I was the one who'd been controlling him. He gave a real performance, making out he was on sedatives and anti-depressants because of *me*, when the truth was he'd been on various combinations of drugs since he was thirteen.

My lawyer tried to convince the court that Lee had been the one controlling *my* life for years. But I wasn't the one with the history of mental illness. I was the one in a 'position of authority and trust', trust I had criminally abused, the judge declared later. Everything was stacked against me. The jury cleared me of attempted murder but found me guilty of grievous bodily harm. The judge gave me seven years. The two baseball cap guys were handed warnings and ordered to pay the cost of replacing Lee's door. My lawyer had the charges of conspiracy against Jade thrown out. A few months later my countercharges were brought against Lee in his own trial. I testified, again giving a full account of everything that had happened. But it was no good. By that point my case had been in the local papers, the jury would have known who I was. I was a head case, a monster. He was given a suspended sentence of twelve months for what he did to me. He's never seen the inside of a prison. Three years later, I'm still here.

So now you know everything. I have debated for weeks whether or not to tell you. I was scared that if I did you wouldn't write to me any more. But you shared your biggest secret with me. It wouldn't be fair if I held mine back now.

I appreciate this is a lot to take in. I'd understand

if you needed some time to process your thoughts. But please do write back soon. Your letters help me.

Ruby

The letter raised a number of questions: How could such a dreadful miscarriage of justice occur without anyone outside of Stoke-on-Trent knowing about it? Was this the whole truth, or was she tricking me?

And then another far more troubling question.

Can I stop this, whatever this is, now?

The letter also made me think of my mother. I remember as a boy overhearing her on the phone saying I was the only thing preventing her from leaving Frank. I felt such guilt over that. Still do. I remember her muffled sobs. The air was so heavy in our bungalow, thick and hot like before a storm. Thinking of it brought that horrible heat back to me. I kicked off the duvet but it was no good. I climbed out of bed and went downstairs for a glass of water. As I drank I was suddenly seized by an irresistible idea. I would google Ruby!

Back in bed I searched. It took a while but eventually I found a hundred words about it in a local paper. The headline:

GUILTY: LOCAL THERAPIST
GETS 7 YEARS

The reporter's account seemed to align with Ruby's. I

didn't learn anything more than what she had chosen to share. Of more interest to me was the photo accompanying the article. Evidently, it had been cropped from a portrait (the photo was credited to Facebook). The caption: *7 years: Ms Holland*. Ruby's mouth is smiling but the slope of her tired eyes betrays her true feelings. Looking into those eyes it was difficult to mistrust what she had told me. She was very beautiful. Her wavy brown hair was tied back but a lock had escaped and hung, like a pincer, on her cheek. Large, clear eyes stared out intently. Full lips softened the grimace of her teeth, transformed it – just about – into a smile.

***

Someone has pushed a note under my door. It says:

>Don't trust G.

I have it here in my pocket. I will dispose of it later. Could the G refer to Gordon? If not him, whom? I don't know any other Gs. But who could want to warn me about Gordon? Gordon is everyone's friend. At least he makes out he is.

I don't recognise the handwriting. The note was clearly written in haste; there's a uniformity to the lettering that can only be achieved when one is writing quickly, from muscle memory. The pencil (a carpenter's, I'd recognise 2H lead a mile off) has dug deep down into the paper and the full stop has pierced all the way through it. Did Robbie write this? If so, where is he and how did he convey it to me?

I knocked again at his door earlier and got no answer. Until I can safely dispose of the note I will hide it where Gordon will not find it should he come around snooping again.

***

Throughout the rest of February and March 2016, Victoria and I settled into a curious new routine: an intricately woven dual schedule designed so we would hardly ever see each other. It was like a ballet; a scene where two lovers, soloing at opposite ends of the stage, cross paths again and again and very nearly but never quite touch. She began spending more time at her parents', often staying the night. But in her absence, I slept like a baby. I spreadeagled in the big bed and because she was not there beside me physically, she faded from my mind.

On one of these nights I wrote again to Ruby. I kept the laptop in the bedroom now. Peculiarly, knowing now what Ruby looked like, having an image of her in my head made the task of writing to her feel somehow different. I found it difficult to start. I typed out half a dozen first lines and discarded them all. I was hesitant, nervous even. But why? I knew what I wanted to say in the letter, roughly what I wanted to convey, but whereas before I could type with abandon now I found myself taking pains over the wording, measuring my language. Was I trying to sound clever? Was I, in crafting my letter, being less honest? Writing to her in bed felt intimate. Victoria was gone. And here with me, in a sense in her place, was Ruby.

Here is what I wrote:

1 March 2016

Dear Ruby

I am humbled that you decided to share your story with me. Do you know where Lee is now? Has he ever tried to contact you in prison?

I once knew a man like Lee. My mother's second husband Frank. He lived with us throughout my adolescence until he died. He used to abuse her. Night after night. Systematically. I saw the marks on her calves, her thighs and arms, her wrists where he'd tied her up.

Frank was a religious man. He talked about Jesus a lot. About Jesus' suffering. The crucifixion. On the day he moved in with us he hung a cross in every room. He went into my father's workshop, grabbed a claw hammer and a box of nails and went around the whole house. The cross in the bathroom was on the back of the door so when you were sat on the toilet you had no choice but to stare at it. My father was devoutly secular. I have hated the idea of religion ever since Frank entered our lives with his prayers that went on for ages at the dinner table, with his King James Bible that he quoted from all the time, with his insistence that Christmas morning was spent at church and not at home with marmalade and best butter on toast opening presents in our pyjamas.

I was just a boy, afraid of him too. Once I told my mother I was going to call someone. She begged me not to, made me promise to say nothing. I had never seen fear like that in a person before.

She used to be so energetic, so bright. She'd throw parties, barbecues in the summer, and my father's family would come to spend a weekend at the seaside with us. Always a glass of wine in her hand. Always a smile. She changed so much when she was with Frank. He shut off her oxygen, her sunlight, and she withered away. To see the person she'd become by the end, a sort of faded photocopy of my mother, holding his hand dutifully at his bedside in hospital, made me so much angrier than the beatings themselves ever did.

Over the years following Frank's death she gradually regained some of her lost colour. But

Frank's reign still cast a shadow. She'd jump at the slightest thing, a toilet flushing, a letter being pushed through the letter slot, a car horn. Frank's bruises had long since disappeared but the psychological marks he left never faded.

The cottage was Frank's. He left it to my mother and she left it to me. But as far as I know she never set foot inside. So there is nothing associated with her inside. No memories, good or painful.

In a sense my mother's dementia was a relief. I liked to believe that she was now living in a world in which Frank didn't exist, the world before they met. I liked to believe that she was – in her head – with my father again. Probably, I thought this to soothe my own guilt.

Dan

PS This town has gone referendum mad. A gazebo has gone up in town and a bunch of old former trawlermen sit on plastic chairs and yell *Let's take back our seas! Let's take back our livelihoods!* through a megaphone and thrust leaflets into people's hands. I don't think I'll vote. I've enough to occupy my mind. At any rate the outcome seems to be a foregone conclusion.

One evening I drove to Vic's parents' house. I parked the

Transporter out of sight around the corner and crouched behind a bush where I had a clear view into their living room. At around ten o'clock, she walked into the living room wearing pyjamas clutching her iPad. Her mother and father, whom I had watched watching telly for two hours, both turned to her. They exchanged some words and then Vic leant down to kiss each of them on the cheek. Then she yawned and left the living room. Seeing her like this allowed me to see her for what she was: a woman in pain. I wanted to rush into the house, to barge upstairs and take her in my arms. To say such nice things to her, to tell her everything would be all right now, that I'd come to my senses and I was sorry and I loved her. But I did not. I could not. Instead I crossed the road, slipped quietly up their driveway and into the back garden. The gate squeaked just as I remembered. I settled myself in a bush at the rear of the lawn and looked up at Vic's bedroom window. The curtains were drawn but there was a light on. At some point, I lost track of the exact time, I saw, through the conservatory windows, Vic's mother go into the kitchen, fix herself a glass of water and plod upstairs to bed. For a while my heart would not stop pounding. But it felt good to watch over Vic like this. Even if she didn't realise I was there, I always was.

I stayed until I was satisfied the whole family was in bed then I walked back to the Transporter and drove slowly home. A terrible sickness swirled in my stomach.

Over the next couple of months Ruby and I wrote to each other many more times. At the height of our correspondence we were writing every other day. After the intensity of our early letters, they became lighter in tone. Long rambling notes. Some a dozen pages long. We talked about everything, and nothing. She told me about her childhood in Stoke. She told me about her patients including a Syrian refugee, a gifted artist, who went on to make a living selling paintings. I told her about my own childhood, my friends, what I was into as a kid. I told her about the time I found a bike wrapped up downstairs on Christmas Eve and how I took it for a spin through the empty streets and how a patrolling policeman found me and drove me home and how my father couldn't hide his pride and amusement. Sometimes whole chunks of text were greyed out, censored, and I wondered what it was she'd tried to say to me, what details had been rubbed out like dirty secrets. I wondered also which parts of my own letters had been redacted and whether these omissions might in some way have skewed the picture she'd assembled of me. She said writing to me made her feel good. I told her the same.

Throughout this time Victoria began contributing to Scott's YouTube channel, silently demonstrating exercises while he explained. She lunges and holds the lunge and Scott crouches beside her and runs his finger in the air along the perpendicular lines of her thigh and shin. *This is the angle you want*, he says. She lies on her back with her hands behind her head and touches an elbow to her bent knee. *When you reach this point, squeeze.*

Ruby's letters were like a drug. I began checking my emails obsessively, refreshing the page over and over. Brazenly, I wrote to her even when Victoria was around. Vic didn't notice. Invariably, she was either in the kitchen filming herself cooking dinner or doing burpees in the back garden. Ruby's outlook, I noticed, was changing. She started talking less about the past and more about the future. She made jokes. She wrote haikus:

Building a new home,
Danny, with a heart of gold,
I want to see it.

Danny, by the sea,
Free and breezy like a bird,
Floating on a draught.

She asked me to describe myself. She painted me but she would not send the portrait unless I OK'd it. Disclosing my personal address was forbidden by Inbox Inmate, for obvious reasons, but there was a safe way through the programme that inmates could convey physical objects to their correspondents if both parties agreed. I wanted badly to see the painting, to see how she imagined me, and considered getting her to send it. But having our relationship cross over from the virtual to the physical felt like a step too far. Inside my computer Ruby was safely contained. Having something in my hands that she had touched would have felt somehow illicit.

Or was I simply afraid of what Vic might do if she ever found it?

By late May, Lanes End was liveable. One day I found a piece of the smashed Charles and Diana plate on the kitchen floor. Diana's head had broken off cleanly. I stood her up on the mantelpiece in the sitting room. After a bit of minor surgery the grandfather clock began to work again. Its ticking gave the cottage a pulse. I put it in the sitting room opposite Diana. The cottage now had a head and a heart.

I officially converted the smaller of the two out-buildings into my new workshop, meaning I now never worked at Beryl Avenue. It felt good to work at Lanes End, I had more room and more light. Its four square windows looked out onto the clearing, which filled with sunlight like a bowl every afternoon. I worked with the door open and I could hear the wind in the pines and the tide at the bottom of the rocks beyond the pines and occasionally the distant blaring of a foghorn out in Wilder Bay.

One evening, as I was enjoying the peace and the blood-coloured evening sunlight, I realised I still hadn't been inside the shed at the end of the clearing. I grabbed my torch and went over. A broken padlock hung uselessly from the latch. Inside was dark and cool. As I moved I kicked something metallic. I shone the torch at the ground. It was an empty tuna can. I ran my torch in a circle around my feet. More empty cans. Beer bottles. A tattered sheet of tarpaulin hung from four pins in the ceiling. There was a newspaper on the floor. The headline: FIVE MORE DAMNED YEARS. The date: 8 May 2015. Over a year old but too recent to have been Constance Lovett's. Was someone using the shed for shelter? Lanes End was miles from town; why would a vagrant come all the way out here? The cottage was surrounded on three sides by woodland and on the other by the sea. There weren't any villages or settlements anywhere near Lanes End that I was aware of. It would've taken ages to get here from town on foot. *Where are they now?* I thought, sensing suddenly that I was being watched. *Hiding somewhere out of sight in the woods?* I moved swiftly outside and stood in the sun scanning the dark trees, looking intently in every direction, wanting and also not wanting to see something, someone move. But I saw nothing, heard nothing. Warily, with one eye on the treeline, I closed the shed and replaced the padlock.

I told Ruby about the shed. She thought it was

'exciting'. She made up this whole back story about an old man who'd once lived in the cottage as Constance's lover, who'd been thrown out when he had an affair and then, unable to let go, lived in the woods for years keeping watch over her, suffering the pain of seeing other men enter and leave her life, and moving on only after she died a lonely old woman in an unkempt house with overgrown grass.

I decided I wasn't comfortable with the idea of anyone being on my property, not even the postman. So I built a letter box and installed a new gate at the turn-off from the road, farther from the cottage than the original gate. I was busy securing a PRIVATE PROPERTY sign to the gate when I heard a vehicle pull up on the road behind me. Muffled soft rock blared inside it. Then I heard the engine switch off and a door open and slam shut. I turned around and saw the back of a man wearing a waxed jacket and flat cap taking a leak into the bushes beside a muddied old Land Rover. He was still zipping his fly when he turned to face me. He had an inhospitable face, a resting grimace that became even less hospitable when he broke into a smile. I did not return his smile. With a wave he began to approach me, crossing the narrow road without looking. There was no need to look; there were never any cars.

'Howdy!' he called, removing his cap and running

his fingers through greasy hair. He came and stood on the patch of grass beside my new letter box. He put his cap back on and leant casually against it.

'Afternoon.'

'So you're the new owner eh?' He reeked of booze. I nodded. He looked down the lane behind me. 'Lot of land.' I did not respond to his observation. 'I'm sorry, where are my manners? I'm Max. Gray. Allow me to welcome you to the neighbourhood,' he said with a grand sweep of his right arm. He offered me a filthy hand.

'Dan,' I said.

'Pleased to make your acquaintance.' His handshake was limp. His fingers collapsed in my grip like a bundle of flower stems. The repulsive shock of a limp handshake always makes me feel seasick. I relinquished my grip and his hand slithered from mine. 'Did you know Ms Lovett?' he asked. The question completely threw me.

'No.'

'My boys used to bring her farm surplus. Eggs. Milk. Suppose you'll be wanting the same?'

'I'll have to talk to the missus.'

'You local?'

'I'm a Wild' un. Lived here all my life.' He nodded approvingly. Then, after another pause he said, 'Well, I was just driving by and thought I'd pull over and say howdy.'

'It was nice to meet you.'

Gray flashed his small sharp teeth at me, rapped his knuckles against the letter box and walked away. He was halfway across the road when he turned sharply on his heels, holding a finger in the air, and called, 'I almost forgot!' He went to his Land Rover and opened the boot. He climbed fully in and, after some frantic rummaging, came out wielding a long wooden post. A square sign was secured to one end of the post. He dragged it across the road upside down. 'Here you go,' he said, flipping the sign around and holding it up beside him. In large white lettering on a red background it said: LET'S TAKE BACK CONTROL. VOTE LEAVE. 'What do you think? It'd be good here,' he said indicating a spot next to the letter box. He passed the sign to me, removed his cap and began running his grubby fingers through his hair again. 'Private property eh?' he said, looking at my new sign. 'You talk to your missus alright?' Then he got in his Land Rover and drove away.

**

Yesterday I was in the workshop trying to work on your gift. Usually, work carries my mind away. But today all I could see was the note '*Don't trust G*' and Gordon's suspicious fingers in my video player and the black figure running towards the woods. What does it all mean? I don't want to know. I don't want to be involved. I'm tired of mystery.

Perhaps my ultimate weakness is that I care too deeply about others. I assume their pain, like Ruby did. I wring my hands. I get too close. I allowed Ruby to get too close and I have allowed Robbie to do the same. It exposes me. The note is gone now of course, disposed of, but since it arrived I feel like I'm walking through thick fog. I can sense around every corner someone waiting to attack me. And so today, though the bright outdoors beckons, I have not left this room. I have sat here reading Ruby's old letters and feeling the old feelings creep slowly up my body like vines, wrapping around me, squeezing me.

Sleep last night was difficult. But there's a man down the way who makes his own booze. I tried it once. It's disgusting but it's strong. I think I'll pay him a visit.

**

There were only two weeks left on our lease at Beryl Avenue.

Victoria hadn't seen Lanes End since January. One evening, I reminded her as much. She was sat on the couch looking pensively down at her iPad at a photo of herself which she'd spent half an hour altering in various ways; cinching her arms and smoothing her skin until she resembled a grotesque alternate version of herself.

'It's totally different now,' I said. She had begun

working on the gap between her thighs, widening it somehow so that more of the light from behind her shone through.

'When does our lease run out again?' She carried on zooming in and zooming out, tapping and pinching, removing, sanding, reducing, editing her true self from the picture.

'The twenty-sixth. We're moving in on Heritage Day, Saturday the twenty-fifth.'

'You can take me that week.'

'You promise?'

'If it means you'll stop nagging me about it.'

That night a new letter arrived from Ruby. I could see immediately that this letter was different from the ones she'd sent recently. It was a lot shorter for starters, to such an extent that I assumed it had been truncated by some computer glitch. I scrolled to the very bottom, to where it says 'Click here to reply to your Inbox Inmate,' and I caught a glimpse of the last line of the letter, '… please don't hate me' and I knew something was up. I sensed the tectonics of my relationship with Ruby were about to shift. How had I become so perceptive about a woman I'd never met, but lost all sense of connection with Vic?

I have copied out her letter in full below:

6 June 2016

Dear Dan

I've been lying to you.

The version of me that you've been reading in these letters hasn't been entirely true. When we started writing six months ago, I was in a terrible place. I don't cope with life in here as well as I make out. Friendship doesn't exist here, love doesn't exist. No one makes eye contact. Everyone is so guarded. I hoped every morning that I would wake to some calamity, a riot, a suicide, a fire, anything that would break the pattern of petty cruelties, of loneliness. New Year's Eve was particularly hard on me. Jade was meant to visit but couldn't come because of some delay on the motorway. I woke up on the first of January feeling nothing of the renewal of a new year. I felt only a renewed hopelessness. So when I got your angry little letter it jolted me, made me realise that there was still a world out there. Made me realise how I'd slid into despair. So I engaged. I told you stories about my past, about the reason I'm in here. They weren't lies. Where I have been less honest is in my feelings. I feel we've become so close over these past months. You've told me your darkest secrets. I have told you mine. Without your letters I don't know how I would have survived. In my head we are the only two people in this world who are awake, just like Winston and Julia! I feel I can call you my true friend.

I have been surprised though, to find myself thinking of you even when I'm not looking at your letters or writing to you. Though I have only your description of yourself to go on, still I find myself thinking of you. When I'm walking in the yard, I think of you and how nice it would be to walk beside you. When I'm eating in the canteen, I think of you and I picture us talking and laughing over a meal. When I'm lying in my bunk and looking at my painting of you, I think of how I want to touch you, and be touched by you.

I never used to think of the future. It only made things harder. But since we found each other I think of the future now with excitement. I know now that happiness is as simple as loving someone and being loved back for no other reason than that you deserve it. That is the future I envisage for myself. I'm sorry if this comes as a shock to you. And I'm sorry if I have misjudged the situation, but I don't think I have. I know how hard it has been for you too, out there, alone. We both deserve so much better.

I won't be in here forever, Dan. Do you think, one day, I could come to visit you? I would ask no more than friendship from you. If I love you without receiving anything in return it would be a better life than to have never known you at all.

You must think I'm crazy. I nearly deleted this whole thing just now, my finger was hovering over the key. But I have denied my feelings for too long. And I feel you're about to make a terrible mistake. If I don't tell you how I feel now, it will be too late. Please don't hate me.

Ruby

Was it true? Was it even possible? Could a person fall in love with another person simply through letters? I went into Alfred's room, to the open window overlooking the back garden. '... you're about to make a terrible mistake'. Was Ruby right? I had the sense that this thought was already there inside my head, cloaked in some dark corner, and that Ruby had simply shone a light onto it.

Ruby's confession had put me in an agitated state. It was suddenly intolerable to be inside. I ran out of the hot house into the back garden. The sun was setting. The trees were black. Someone somewhere was playing a cello. I took off my shirt and sat on it and pictured Ruby's beautiful, sullen face in the newspaper. I lay back on the grass and its coolness on my skin seemed to snap me into consciousness. I tried to order all the things I knew about her:

She was my friend. She was a criminal.
She had painted me and written poems for me. She had nearly killed a man.
She was beautiful. She was dangerous.
She loved me.

This last thought stood alone. There was nothing to prove that she didn't love me. It must be true, I thought. She loved me. 'I know how hard it has been for you too, out there, alone,' she had written.

My body trembled with strange energy. I sat up and felt the warm air against my back, which was damp with sweat. Was I shaking with gratitude, excitement, or fear? This was a test, I decided. I could not allow my head to be turned by a character in a story. Because when you boiled it down, that was all Ruby was. Words on a screen, a photograph in a newspaper. Our relationship was virtual.

I remained in the garden a while longer, listening to the dark melody of the cellist. The music seemed to rise out of the very earth itself. Its deep notes rose ominously up into the darkening sky.

**

I knock on Robbie's door every day after lunch. I call his name. I linger. I listen. I never get a response or hear movement. Today there were voices. Two. One of them was much louder, deeper than the other. I did not knock. I stood and pressed an ear gently to the door. The louder voice was angry, sharp. The quieter voice – Robbie's I presumed – spoke only in timid mono-syllables. I strained my ears but I could not recognise the louder voice. A couple of guys walking by saw me bent at Robbie's door. I straightened up as they passed. Our eyes met. They shot me a suspicious glare. One of them was familiar to me. Where have I seen him before? When they were gone I pressed my ear back to the door. Now silence. It occurred to me that the voices might be listening for listeners. If I moved at all I'd have given myself away. I had no choice but to remain still. I closed my eyes. I slowed my breathing. And then, suddenly, the sound of something large and metal smashing to the ground. The louder voice launched into another dia-tribe. Its tone indicated the interview was coming to an end. I had to move now or risk being caught. I walked away, briskly, as far from Robbie's door as my feet could carry me. I sat and rested while my heart slowed. When I had a moment to think I of course assumed that the louder voice belonged to Gordon. But then I saw Gordon, out on his daily stroll, talking with people and smiling, nowhere near mine or Robbie's. So who was it? Is Gordon not 'G' after all? I have no idea what's going on any more, Lucy.

***

I stopped writing to Ruby. Went cold turkey.

Months of constant contact, mutual support, affection even, and then poof, nothing. Gone. I could've written her a short note; *I'm sorry, I can't do this any more*, or just quit the programme entirely; at least that would have sent a clearer message. But I couldn't bear the thought of never seeing her letters again. I read them over and over. They had offered me such comfort. They had guided me to the other side of a raging sea that had tried to push me down and drag me to the bottom. But in doing so they had served their purpose. Victoria and I would soon be leaving this place. It no longer mattered what I felt for Ruby. Just as it didn't matter any more what Ruby felt for me.

But the letters continued.

10 June 2016

Dear Dan

I've been trying to remind myself over the past few days that you're busy moving house, getting things ready. *Give the man a break*, I thought, *be patient*. It took all my willpower not to write again yesterday. *You're being stupid Ruby*, I told myself, *a silly teenager; he'll write soon enough*. But today is day four. You haven't taken this long to reply since

February. Today when I logged in and saw that you still hadn't written I couldn't help myself.

I don't regret telling you how I felt. But if you don't feel the same way please don't punish me. My life consists only of punishment. I don't need another layer of it. If you haven't written because you don't know what to say, or because you're afraid of saying the wrong thing, just know that you can't say anything wrong. I just want you to be honest.

I hope you write soon.

Ruby

I sat for hours that night with the laptop open, my fingers twitching above the keys. I could sense her pain and I knew that in just a few keystrokes I could obliterate it. I focused on the telly, on the football match unfolding on it. I sat and watched the players – the French in blue, the Romanians in yellow – run around after the little white dot. It was soothing: the constant drone of the crowd rising and falling in time with the action, the hypnotic movement of the ball across the screen in graceful arcs. Super slow-motion close-ups of players' faces revealed expressions of anguish, frustration, ecstasy. I envied the simplicity of the game. I wanted to be like those men: only one thing on their unfettered minds. Picture the goal, I told myself, think only of scoring. When the match was over I knew I would never write to her again.

The next day there was another letter.

11 June 2016

Dear Dan

It suddenly occurred to me last night that something may have happened to you. *What if he's lying in a ditch somewhere in his van, what if he's in hospital and he physically can't get to a computer to write to me?* I felt like a fool for being so impatient. I felt so ashamed. I couldn't sleep thinking of you. But then it was this same thought that brought me solace. I don't want you to be hurt, Dan – I never want that – but the thought of you being somehow prevented from writing to me is so much easier to accept than you choosing not to.

Please write back soon.

Ruby

And another the next day:

12 June 2016

Dan

I'm starting to think I conjured you up. You're my creation. Last night I looked at your portrait on my wall, into your dark eyes, and I whispered to you:

Are you real? You did not answer of course. You're very quiet lately. Tell me Dan: Are you real? Who do I love? Where is this love going to? Where has it been going to all this time? I'm desperate. Please just give me a sign.

Please write. I'm sorry. I'm going out of my mind.

Ruby

And the next:

13 June 2016

Dan

Why did I end my last letter with an apology? I'm NOT sorry. You're the one who should be sorry. It's been a whole week since I told you how I felt, since I laid myself out before you like a newspaper. How could you do this to me? I'm so humiliated. I know you're getting these messages. You could end my suffering with one word. I don't even care now if that word is 'no'. I just can't stand this silence any more.

Ruby

And again:

14 June 2016

I laughed today. I knew there'd be nothing from you again, and I was right. So I laughed.

You're cruel. Heartless. I'm swinging on your hook and you don't even have the courage to put me out of my misery. I can't stand that I still have this hope inside me. It brings me down here to this overheated computer room to log on, to look at your old letters. All the other girls type away furiously, their tongues poking out like dogs. I wish I could go back to being like them. I wish I could go back in time; I would never have written back to you. The numbness of before was far better than this burning pain I feel throughout my whole body now. I hope one day you look back at these letters from me and you feel regret.

I hope you suffer how I am suffering.

Ruby

And finally:

15 June 2016

Dan

How has it come to this? How can a person be one thing and then the next day something else: nothing?

This is the last you'll ever hear from me. You're no better than him.

Ruby

PS Victoria is going to leave you.

It was a suicide vest of a letter. She meant to hurt me with it. The confidence of the statement frightened me. It was an unwavering stare into the camera. She is going to leave you. She is. Not a warning; a foretelling.

What lingered most was the feeling I had made a dangerous enemy. Look what happened to the last man to cause her pain, I thought. I reassured myself that she had no idea where I lived. Apart from that it was somewhere coastal in the Northwest of England, my address was unknown to her. Plus, by the time she was released – which wasn't for another three years – her rage would have subsided, she'd have another me, another outlet. Maybe I was just the latest in a long line of men she'd become entangled with online. Perhaps I wasn't so unique a figure in her life after all.

But still at night I started dreaming of a man lying at the bottom of a flight of stairs, his broken legs bent back at the hips. And in the dreams, as I knelt over that broken body, I could sense her presence.

The next day Victoria agreed to see Lanes End. I picked her up in the Transporter from work and drove east out of town. With the setting sun behind us, Wilder became silhouetted in my rear-view: a mouth filled with crooked blackened teeth.

'Here we are,' I said as I rounded the bend of the lane onto the clearing. The low sun shone a spotlight on the front of the cottage. I got out of the Transporter and let her in the side door. She walked ahead of me slowly, opening each door just enough to poke her head inside.

'Why don't you use the front door?' she asked later.

'You can if you prefer.' I handed her the keys.

She unlocked the front door and surveyed the clearing. I felt then, as I looked at her silhouette in the doorway, that we would be happy here. She stepped outside and I heard a sound like glass breaking. I went outside and saw that a pint of milk had been placed on the step. She'd knocked it over and globules of milk had spilt onto the shale. A tray of eggs had been placed next to it, half of which were smashed.

'Fucking Gray,' I said under my breath.

'What are those doing there?'

'I don't know,' I lied.

On the drive home Victoria began rooting frenziedly through the glove compartment.

'What are you after?' I asked.

'A charger.' She held her lifeless phone in her hand

and pressed its one button over and over as though trying to resuscitate it.

'I don't have a smartphone,' I reminded her.

When we got home she rushed through to the living room and plugged her phone in. I went into the kitchen and poured myself a glass of water. After a few moments I heard the phone's text notification tone go off multiple times. Ding. Ding. Ding. I went upstairs to begin packing for the move, and to distract my mind. As I passed the living room door I saw her typing away rapturously, her feet curled up beside her on the couch. Outside the light was fading, the day finally ending.

Over the next few days Victoria packed too. She refused to do this with me present. She said she needed space and that I 'got in the way'.

There were precisely three photographs in the house. They had all been stood up in frames to the right of the telly the entire four and a half years we'd lived there. One was of Vic's parents on holiday. The second photo was of my mother. It was taken at the old bungalow in the kitchen. Post-Frank. She is mid stride, marching towards the camera in her Sunday apron, her eyebrows raised and her right index finger pointed in mock warning. Probably I had tried to steal a Yorkshire pudding. Her lips are pursed, on the verge of saying something, no doubt an admonishment. But she looks happy. This was how I liked to remember her.

The third photo was of me and Vic. We are stood outside a church. I am holding a little girl's pink toy umbrella over both of us. Vic is wearing a long dark green dress. Her shoulders are hunched slightly against the cold but she is smiling. I on the other hand look positively aloof. I am thinking only of getting out of the weather. I am not thinking of the woman stood next to me, who loves me, who is pressing into me for warmth. I used to hate that picture but Vic liked it because of the way her dress fitted. Now I couldn't bear to take it down.

The evening of Thursday 23 June 2016 was balmy. There was almost no wind. Occasionally a little gust would blow in your face and die and then another gust would blow on the back of your head as though the wind couldn't make up its mind.

Everything was packed. Everything was ready to go, except the telly. We still needed the telly. It was the fulcrum of the house. Without it we might have had to talk to each other. We sat on the couch with takeaway pizza and watched *Friends* in silence. At about half past ten Vic got a text and insisted we put on the news. She changed the channel. The anchor said: *Let's go now to Gibraltar where I understand they are about to declare the first result of the night…* Suddenly my eyes felt heavy. I craved sleep. *The total number of ballot papers counted was …* I yawned. I rubbed my eyes, missed the numbers. I was so tired. The broadcast returned to the studio. The anchor said: *So there you have it; Gibraltar votes to remain in the European Union. Stay with us for all the reaction from the …* The channel switched back to *Friends*. Vic was back in her usual position, curled away from me, feet tucked beneath her body, phone face down on the arm of the couch. I took the pizza boxes into the kitchen. I looked back at her from the doorway. A burst of canned laughter erupted from the telly. I looked left into the hallway and watched the light alternate white, then red, then white, then red, depending on whether Chandler or Monica spoke. There was no other light left. I heard the channel change again, back to the news. I stood in the living room doorway for a few moments watching. A grey man said, *If this kind of result is replicated across the country it could be a very long and bloody night indeed for Leave.*

'I'm going up,' I said.

'OK. I'm going to watch a bit more.'

'Night,' I said, turning to leave.

'Dan?' Vic said softly behind me.

'Yes?'

She did not immediately say anything. I looked into her eyes and smiled. Then she did something she hadn't done in more than a year and a half. She touched me. She reached out a hand and, stretching over the arm of the couch, brushed my hip tenderly with the tips of her fingers.

'Goodnight, Dan,' she said. My eyes suddenly filled with tears. If I spoke I'd crack. I went upstairs and climbed into bed feeling that everything was going to be OK.

Everything was packed. Everything was ready to go. Everything was fine.

The next morning Vic had already left for her morning run. I went downstairs to make a cup of tea. It was Friday, 24 June 2016 and tomorrow we would leave this place and start again. It seemed I had awoken into a new era. I felt light, unencumbered. I turned on the telly. *Friends* was still showing, seemingly as always. I looked over to where Vic had been sitting, to where she'd reached out to me. I hadn't imagined it. Her seashell imprint in the couch was indelible. *Friends* finished, and in the ad break I channel-hopped. There was a niggling thought in the back of my mind. I flipped back to *Friends* but *Friends* wasn't on. It was something else. Another programme! A theme song I'd never heard, characters I didn't know. I looked ahead in the schedule for the next episode of *Friends*. But there was no more *Friends* for the rest of the day.

The house was empty and quiet. I was deeply agitated. Alfred was fluttering crazily in his cage. I began pacing up and down the living room. I looked out onto Beryl Avenue. There were no people anywhere. No cars. I turned to BBC News and watched it with the sound off, not taking anything in, just looking at it. BBC News calmed me. The slow-moving text across the red ticker, the sensible-looking man looking directly into my eyes, the hazy figures of people moving industriously behind him. The words passing along the bottom of the screen started coming into focus. POUND FALLS TO LEVELS NOT SEEN SINCE 1985. PRIME MINISTER DUE TO MAKE STATEMENT SHORTLY. I was comprehending the words but not understanding them. VOTE IS A ROAR OF DEFIANCE AGAINST WESTMINSTER. Frozen with the remote in my hand, the scale of what had transpired overnight began to dawn on me. FTSE FALLS 7 PER CENT IN MINUTES AS MARKETS OPEN. Where was Victoria? Did she know? Something felt terribly wrong. The prime minister appeared on-screen outside Number Ten. I unmuted the telly. Gravely, he began to speak. The prime minister's wife stood apart from him, off to the side. I heard a strangely familiar sound outside, deep and thunderous, but I did not look to see what it was, I could not break my gaze from the prime minister's ashen, disconsolate face. I heard the front door open.

'Dan.' I heard Victoria's voice in the doorway.

I did not look to her. 'Have you seen this?'

'Dan,' she repeated.

'There are times when it is right to ask the people themselves,' said the prime minister.

'I can't believe it,' I said.

'Dan, we need to talk.'

'Head, heart and soul. I held nothing back,' the prime minister insisted.

'What's going to happen now?' I said.

'Dan, I'm not coming with you tomorrow.'

'This is not a decision I have taken lightly,' said the prime minister. I had heard Vic's words but they were muffled, as though she were in another room.

'I'm leaving you.'

'There's no need for a precise timetable today,' said the prime minister.

'I'm going to live with Scott.' The camera zoomed slowly out to a wider shot to take in the prime minister's wife. She looked on the verge of breaking down, and it was only the sight of this, of another person's sadness, that triggered my own emotions. I felt heat building up behind my eyes. I was still staring at the telly. Vic was stood behind me in the doorway. 'Aren't you going to say anything?' The prime minister's wife reached out towards him. The gesture, the way she held her hand out in the air towards him, like a mother waiting at the school gates for her son, was the same gesture Victoria had made last night. They disappeared into Number Ten, the prime minister rubbing tender circles into the small of his wife's back. I understood now that Victoria's touch was 'goodbye'.

Rooted to the spot, I watched the horror unfurl on the telly while Vic made repeated trips up and down the stairs to fetch her suitcases and boxes. 'Dan?' she said after a time, I have no idea how long, 'The TV?' Finally, I looked at her. Why was she asking me about the TV? 'The TV is mine.' She gently removed the remote from my grip.

My trembling fingers stayed open, caged around nothing. She unplugged the telly and then with some difficulty carried it away. I heard the boot of a car close outside. Moments later she came back into the living room. I was still motionless, mouth agape, quite insensible. 'Are you going to be alright?' she said. A vision of her appearing from the dancing crowd that first Christmas Eve came back to me. My breaths became shallow and rapid. I closed my eyes and the memory played in reverse; she receded into the crowd. I opened my eyes and watched her remove her house key from the keyring and place it on the coffee table. Then she left and I heard the coupé fire up outside. I don't remember anything after that. I have no recollection of the rest of that day.

At ten the next morning – moving day – the landlord came to collect the keys.

Not long after, I was in the Transporter and driving away, finally, unhappily, from Beryl Avenue with Alfred beside me, his shrouded cage strapped into the passenger seat.

The traffic into Wilder town centre was unseasonably heavy. It was hot and sticky in the van and I had to crack a window open. I heard the sound of faraway whistles and tooting horns. I looked in my rear-view and noticed that the car behind me was decorated with coloured tinsel and paper. A Union Jack had been tied to the bonnet.

It was Wilder Heritage Day. I had completely forgotten. The town bustled with people like it never did for the 364 other days of the year. The street was lined from the promenade all the way east towards the edge of town and the marina with gazebos and tables, people serving cakes, orange juice and beer. I could hear a brass band and pounding dance music and both above and beneath them the unintelligible and disorienting sound of three and a half thousand clamouring voices. I rolled slowly along the high street, piercing through the crowd like a boat through thick swampland. People were walking in the road, touching the Transporter with their hands as I passed them. A group of costumed girls danced an Irish jig in front of Poundland. A police horse was being petted on its nose by a group of children and moving backwards in jittery circles while its handler tried to soothe it. A lamppost had been dressed as a maypole and around it a group of men clad in traditional English white pranced and leapt.

I heard something slam violently into the Transporter. I looked up to see the swaying figure of Max Gray. A half-smoked cigarette hung from his mouth. He was clutching a can of Special Brew in one hand and a blue carrier bag in the other. He held his can aloft like a trophy. His eyes were closed. He seemed to be dancing to some music inside his head. The ash on his cigarette was an inch long. It began to dawn on me that he didn't recognise me; that he hadn't slammed my bonnet in salutation but simply because my bonnet was there. Eventually, he staggered off the road and onto the pavement, tripping over the kerb. A pair of lanky boys followed after him. One was wearing a tracksuit, the other jeans and Union Jack T-shirt. The one in the tracksuit, the smaller one, spat on the road in front of the Transporter.

After Gray I felt shaken. Alfred flapped inside his cage, perhaps in protest at the noise and the heat. The sky shimmered and vibrated with a superabundance of energy. People dabbed their foreheads, the elderly with handkerchiefs and tissues, the young with the bottoms of their T-shirts or their sleeves. The Fire Service had set up an antique fire engine outside the station and were spraying a fine mist over the street. Topless children ran through its rainbow arc squealing. The firewomen and firemen were clad in full uniform but had peeled the top half of them down like bananas.

I turned left towards the marina. Here the crowd was even thicker. I saw the spot where my father used to park his van and point out the boats as they passed by. The now-defunct RNLI station rose above the marina. On its balcony, as was tradition, an appointed old and snow-bearded man announced each passing vessel. Without exception every boat flew a Union flag. *Here's Reg Turner aboard the Princess of the Sea*, said the old man. *Reggie has been campaigning against the CFP for decades. Everyone, show your appreciation for good old Reg. Give him a round of applause.* The crowd clapped. Then the old man began to shout: *No longer will our livelihoods be dictated to by fat cats in Brussels! No longer will the likes of Reggie and his family suffer because of anti-British laws. We told Brussels we want our seas back! And that's what we're gonna get!* A roar went up around the marina. The people lining the edge of the water produced, almost in unison, little paper Union flags and started waving them hysterically about their heads. This happened for each boat. I had no idea the people of Wilder even cared. But apparently, after all, they did. And they were frenzied in their emotion. They waved their flags and bounced their babies as if we'd just won some glorious victory. I didn't care like they did. I didn't feel like they did. In that moment I had no feelings, my nerves had been sanded down and cauterised. I could only gawp at these people as at strange exotic creatures in a zoo. This joy on their faces, this display, this turnout. It was unfathomable to me. These people were inscrutable. I rolled out of town away from the horns and the whistles and the klaxons and the voices, like a loner leaving a party early.

I was alone in taking the left turn into the country lanes. Everyone else went right.

The relative silence of the countryside was intense. The trees were lush, the fields pregnant and swaying. The cows kneeled in shade and moved their full mouths in slow circles.

As I approached the turn-off to Lanes End I spotted a yellow sign by the gate. It said: SAVE OUR COUNTRYSIDE. SAY NO TO FRACKING. I stopped to open the gate. I checked my new mailbox. It was empty. I drove along the lane through the woods and pulled up on the shale. Clutching Alfred's cage by the handle I went to the front door. The sun was hot on my back. A gust of sea wind flared and the tall trees surrounding the cottage made sounds like conspiratorial whispers.

***

Today was the last day of September. Robbie came back. He just flounced in and switched the telly on. I was slightly overcome at the sight of him. He sat with his back to the wall. *Still writing letters?* he said, totally deadpan. *You're so old-fashioned. Don't know why you don't just pick up the phone.* His face was covered in bruises, cuts, welts. His right eye was swollen shut. It wept constantly. I asked Robbie everything. He did not answer any of my questions. I told him I had been looking for him, that I had been worried about him. He would not engage except when I rose from my chair to announce that I was going to report his assault. He leapt from my bed and pleaded with me not to. He pulled at my sleeves and prevented me from leaving the room. The fear in his eyes reminded me so much of my mother when I was a teenager and she stopped me from going to the police over Frank. It disarmed me and I fell heavily back into my chair. Clearly, he's suffered a significant trauma and I will have to be patient with him. I promised him I wouldn't report it. I calmed him, got him to sit back down on the bed. His left eye had wept a shiny trail all down his face. I fetched him some more tissues. He looked so pathetic forming one into a soft point and dabbing it into his eye. Watching him, I was moved. He was like a child.

I wonder if you have read my first letter.

Lucy, I am getting now to the bit you must be waiting

for and dreading. I promise to leave nothing out. I will simply replay everything in my head and transcribe what I hear. It is time now for bed, I am writing this by moonlight. I will start again tomorrow, in October. Affectionately yours

D

3

OCTOBER

October 2033

Dear Lucy

In four weeks the clocks go back. *Spring forward, fall back*. That means I have four weeks left of British Summer Time. Four weeks before the nights draw in. And shortly after that, as if emboldened by the darkness, Halloween.

It was never a significant occasion for me growing up. I remember once, I was six or seven, wandering the streets with a toy joinery set attached to my father's utility belt: saw, hammer, spirit level, pencil behind my ear. I jangled plastically through our streets knocking on doors. One person came to the door and said 'trick' and I didn't have a clue what to do. I had no tricks. I just walked to the next house bemused.

Everyone thinks Halloween is a bit of fun: a childish

parade. But Ruby took it more seriously than that. Ruby taught me its true meaning. It is actually meant to be the time of year we remember the dead, the saints and the martyrs. Now every Halloween I make sure to remember mine. The dead (little Daniel), the saints (Father), the martyrs (Mother).

Robbie's weeping eye seems to be getting worse. I said he should see a doctor. He waved my concern away but he's begun talking about his great love Maud again, which I take as an encouraging sign. Yesterday, apart from his battered and discoloured appearance, there was something deeply unsettling about his persona, about the way he ignored my questions. He's hiding something, I'm certain of it.

**

It was sometime in the middle of July before I experienced the conscious thought: this is now my home. I was down by the rock pools, at the bottom of what I had come to think of as the cliff, behind Lanes End. I was wearing the waxed jacket, the one I had found hanging up in the corridor, which I wore now always. I had a pocket full of shells and a pocket full of pebbles. The tide was out. I bent down to look into one of the pools of water and I saw my newly bearded reflection and I thought: this is me, this is my home.

Sometimes the sea rose all the way up the cliff and

when I slept with the bedroom window open I could hear it dashing itself against the rocks. I looked out across the flat wet sand. The sea receded so far from the shore here that I sometimes doubted its return. The peaks of the Lake District, hazy and lilac on the horizon, and the great bay gave me a sense of security, of insulation, but also of melancholy. I came down here often to trawl through these rock pools for shells and pebbles, though I wasn't sure why. I liked the smell of the rock pools and the way the landscape looked peaceful, deathly quiet as in the aftermath of some great natural disaster or war. In the whole time I'd been living here I had never once seen another person.

I went back towards the cottage. I climbed barefoot from rock to rock, right and then left, to get back up the cliff. I found my boots, with socks neatly balled inside them, at the top. When I had put them back on I went through the trees and entered the cottage by the back door into the kitchen. Alfred was standing on the kitchen table.

'You're up,' I remarked. And then it came to me. 'Look what I've got,' I said, and showed him a handful of the shells from my left pocket. 'Come on!' I went through into the nursery where I had installed his cage and upended my pockets onto the floor in a pile. 'Look at those!' Alfred had followed me obediently into the nursery and was inspecting the haul, leaping and stooping around it. He liked to arrange them into displays on the floor. His favourite specimens made it to the floor of his cage, which I left open. He was free to wander around the cottage as he pleased. I had initially opened his cage in a fit of petulant self-destructive pity. 'Go, like all the rest!' I urged. 'Go on! Piss off you murderous little bastard!' But Alfred never left. I could leave all the windows and doors open and he still never left. Now we were friends.

Victoria had taken everything with her. I used Constance Lovett's things now. I owned nothing apart from my tools in the workshop and my clothes, and apart from what I had installed during the renovations (fridge, cooker) there was no technology whatsoever at Lanes End. I lived in an austere and antiquated way surrounded by old-fashioned furniture and using old-fashioned things. The stovetop kettle's whistle sounded like a train arriving. Constance's cutlery was basic and slightly stained. Her crockery on the other hand seemed too fine to use on a daily basis and so I took all of my meals from the same blue bowl. I left the rest as they were, wrapped up in newspaper in the plastic cartons in the box room. Those cartons were a trove. A lifeline. They saved me from half a dozen trips to the shops and encounters with people, which I was at pains to avoid. I was content in my isolation. Gray's eggs and milk surplus carried on appearing. He just left them on the grass by the gate. Sometimes only a couple of eggs, sometimes the full complement. Once or twice just milk. Never an accompanying note. I accepted them happily and without question. I walked up the lane with the waxed jacket over the top of my pyjamas and bent down and hooked them towards me through the slats in the fence, quickly, in case someone should be out there waiting to, God forbid, speak to me.

I fantasised about Scott dying. I pictured him being crushed beneath his own weights. Arrogantly lifting more than he was able: the bar would descend like a slow-motion guillotine towards his heaving chest. The bar rolled backwards from his crushed ribs – a deadly rolling pin – onto his neck, and his legs would flail and kick like a fly sprayed with insecticide. In my head the scene played out like a snuff film, a grainy YouTube clip. It went viral, it was a sensation.

One day I discovered a telephone in one of the cartons and plugged it into the wall socket in the criss-crossing corridors. I knew I would have to rejoin the flow of society one day; I couldn't live like this forever. But as I heard the dialling tone I knew I wasn't ready yet. Society would have to wait.

I spent a lot of time outdoors. There was marshland beyond the rock pools and I would head aimlessly into its infinite expanse. If I walked far enough west I could make out Wilder on the horizon. That was the point at which I always turned back. Other times I walked through the woods that surrounded the house. There was no purpose to those walks. I spent a lot of time just wandering about in the waxed jacket. I would go to great lengths to avoid getting in the Transporter and driving to the little shop on the road into Wilder. I found an apple tree and for a whole week ate nothing but stewed apples and sugar for breakfast and scrambled eggs for dinner. I lost weight. I bent over in front of the bathroom mirror once and pinched the folds of my belly skin between my thumb and fingers and felt it disappear as I straightened up. I let my hair and beard grow.

Ruby's fiction about Constance's ex-lover keeping a silent vigil over the cottage kept creeping into my thoughts and preventing sleep. I couldn't shake the thought that there was someone out there, a man, hiding amongst the trees, at the edge of the clearing, between the outbuildings, by the back door. Just standing. Watching. Every night he reappeared in my thoughts. Unable to sleep I would climb out of bed and stare at the trees and the bushes, sometimes for an hour or more. Conditioned by years of alarms I still woke early each day. As a consequence, during those first few months at Lanes End, I slept hardly at all.

One night I had an accident. There was a powerful

storm. I have always been mesmerised by heavy rain. I can watch it for hours. Ever since I was a kid. I went to the bedroom window and stared out across the clearing. I felt an urge to be out there in it. I stamped into my boots and dashed outside, leaving the front door open behind me. My sense of direction was obliterated. It was so loud. I felt like I was stood next to some massive churning machine. A yellow fork lit up the sky and I ran into the trees to await the thunder. After a few seconds it sounded somewhere far off, deep and guttural, like an animal growling a warning. The rain was unrelenting. It seemed an impossible amount of water was falling from the sky. But I could not go back inside yet. I was manic and I went deeper into the narrow band of trees and down towards the cliff and the fields of reeds beyond where I had not yet explored. I pressed on through the darkness skipping from stone to stone, running, pumping my arms. I could see nothing, except when the lightning returned to cast a strobe across the landscape. The terrain was uneven. I was moving too quickly. I snagged my foot on a rock and felt my body twisting, falling. I groped at the air. Right before my body made contact with the ground I experienced the sickening realisation that I was going to hurt myself. Then my body met the ground, and consciousness was shaken from my mind upon impact.

When I came to, I felt intense heat in my left knee

like it had been doused in oil and set alight. I heard the distant sounds of motorcycle engines or lawn-mowers or chainsaws. Also: a foghorn, birdcall and an aeroplane like a great finger scoring a fold in the sky. I rolled onto my side and I prised open my eyes carefully, allowing the tiniest amount of light to enter. It was daytime. I had been lying here all night. My legs were submerged in water and the tide was coming in. I stood up, hunched and clam-eyed, and surveyed the scene before me. Marshland. I found myself amongst green reeds, luminous like Alfred's plumage against the grey sky. In front of me the great bay opened up like a pair of arms offering an embrace to the open sea. I planted my feet wide and turned slowly to face the land behind me. My left knee complained with each movement; I didn't dare inspect it yet. Fields stretched towards the horizon, rising and dipping in curved troughs. The sun shone through a hole in the clouds and caused a golden disc to move across the land like a spotlight. In a distant field away to my left stood a tiny cluster of stone buildings. Two very close together and a third set apart. I did not detect any life. No smoke rose from the chimneys and the windows were not lit. I hoped the buildings were uninhabited; an abandoned old farmstead. I wasn't in the mood for neighbours.

The knee was problematic. But the greatest source of discomfort was the shivering cold sickness that had seized my body. As I shambled through the pines towards the back door of the cottage – after a long struggle getting back up the rocks – I could feel my body giving in. A deathly sleep was coming. Leaning against the cottage's walls I inched my way around to the front door, which was wide open. A great oval of grass in the centre of the clearing was waterlogged and reflected the morning sky like a mirror. Hopping along the corridor on my one good leg I somehow made it to my bed.

I awoke and it was night again. I could feel a breeze and remembered that the front door was still open. It had been open now for an entire night and day. But it was too far. I could not move my body. Alfred chirped incessantly. He was hungry too. I fell back asleep.

The next morning my stomach dragged me into the kitchen. I ate oats with water and put a handful of Alfred's food in the middle of the kitchen table. After this I sat on the floor of the kitchen and wriggled out of my still-damp pyjamas. I looked to my right and could just about make out the faint outline of the mouse's dead body that I thought I had bleached away.

I was very unwell. Victoria began invading my dreams. She and Ruby conspired in whispers. They each wore prison garb and shielded their mouths with coned hands so I could not read their lips. They giggled and flourished their hair like teenagers. In half-sleep, when

I had one hand on the wheel of my own imagination, they came to me more benevolently. Now smiling, now comforting. They both made love to me. Ruby's body was Victoria's old body.

Once I had exhausted the oats I knew I had to make a trip to the supermarket for provisions. There was no other food left and I couldn't have gone foraging with my damaged knee. I drove out slowly along the lane. Each time I squeezed the clutch I emitted a little involuntary wheeze of pain.

Leaning my weight onto my trolley I shambled through the aisles. I could sense people staring at me. I was limping badly on the knee but it was not that which drew their attention. I had not washed in days. My last contact with water had been the tide. My hair was wild, my beard out of control. The waxed jacket was filthy. I saw a woman who looked like Victoria. She was wearing luminously coloured exercise gear and marched with great purpose towards me. I could not run. All I could do was turn away and hope she didn't notice me. I became acutely conscious then of the smell I was emitting. It wasn't her but I had been given a fright. I found myself then watching the other people in the store, observing them with fascination. I was drawn to this human behaviour like a jealous ghost. I suddenly longed to be amongst them, to rejoin them.

When I returned to Lanes End I found two letters in the mailbox. The anti-fracking sign had blown over. I did not stand it back up. I was very hungry. I drank three glasses of water from the kitchen tap one after the other, ate three slices of bread straight from the packet and took two anti-inflammatories. I took a bath and watched the dirt float away from my body on the surface of the water. After the bath I stood staring at my reflection in the mirror. My face was buried beneath clumps of wet dark hair. I took a towel to it, which brought out the specks of white and grey that had recently started coming through, and I realised I looked just like Frank. I was missing only a pair of glasses. This was his property. He must have been here, spent time here. I felt I could sense his presence. In the air. In the walls. I shaved the beard off hurriedly, as if exorcising Frank's spirit. I watched the last of the stubble go down the plughole and then used one of Constance's ornate brushes to tame my hair. Then I sat at the kitchen table and opened the letters. They had both been forwarded on from Beryl Avenue; I hadn't given my address out to anybody apart from Royal Mail. One was junk. The other was a handwritten letter, a job offer from the owner of an online furniture company. A Polaroid of a large storage trunk I had made some years before was enclosed. I remembered it well: mango wood, distressed finish, iron trimmings, fitted with an old-fashioned hasp and staple lock. The owner explained how he loved my work, that many people had enquired about the trunk in his home, that he knew he could sell them in decent quantities through his site for eleven or twelve hundred, of which I'd get five. All materials would be provided, all I had to do was drive to the timber merchant to collect them and he would arrange collection of the finished products. Though I owned the cottage outright I still needed an income. This seemed like the perfect job. The trunks were easy to make. I could make at least three or four per month. I decided to accept.

Once I'd put the rest of the shopping away I went into the box room and retrieved the telephone. I plugged it into the wall socket in the corridor and dialled the number on the brochure. 'Please remember, sir, in some cases it can take up to a week for your account to activate,' said the voice in the call centre.

But an hour later I was live. I was connected. Annoyingly, the signal from the router (which I had to plug in in the only working phone socket I could find on the property, in the larger of the two outbuildings – evidently a garage – as the socket in the corridor turned out to be 'internet dead') only reached to the workshop, the cottage wasn't close enough. So I set up my old laptop on the bench in my workshop and powered it up. I felt suddenly nervous. Avoiding the news and social media, I opened my emails. There were dozens of junk messages.

Offers to enlarge my bank account, my pension, my penis. I deleted them all. When I got down to it there was only one genuine item of mail. It was from Inbox Inmate. My heart leapt violently in my chest as I clicked on the message. This is what she had written:

31 July 2016

Dan

Last night I dreamt you were dead. You were lying on the ground and you had drowned. It felt real. I thought I could smell the sea.

Ruby

I slammed the laptop shut and hobbled quickly back into the cottage and locked the door behind me. The internet was a mistake; I had brought bad magic to Lanes End. I was suddenly freezing cold and I spent the rest of that night on a rocking chair, wrapped in a blanket with my feet tucked beneath me, feeling my weight shift minutely backwards and forwards, and listening to the ticking of the grandfather clock and the snapping of the burning logs.

***

After the summer madness, things have settled down here. The sun has disappeared behind a duvet of clouds.

I haven't seen it in many days. The sun's departure seems to have drawn the energy from people. I am able now to write a great deal. Gordon seems less preoccupied too. I saw him yesterday. He asked me about the mirror frame. I said it was going well and that he should come look at it himself. He said he might. He asked about Robbie. I said he was doing OK and asked Gordon if he knew what had happened. He told me about a fish he caught over the weekend: a catfish. I said I didn't think we had catfish in this country. He laughed and said we're surrounded by water.

Robbie is more talkative than ever. But now I don't find it off-putting. Lately, his anecdotes seem to be taking on an autobiographical tone. They seem to have chronology. At present, in his autobiography, he is a young man. He has been telling me the story of how he met his wife Maud. He stole her from another man, I understand. Another miner from Maltby.

***

I thought I had purchased the router with the intention of rejoining society, of jumping back into its bracing current and allowing it to carry me off. But all I used it for was to buy things. I started buying books and having them shipped to the big Tesco where it was possible to collect them. All the books I could remember my father having read. I didn't read any of them. I was afraid to. I can't really explain why. Opening the front covers made me cringe, like lifting a rock to see the writhing worms and insects clinging to it. I read the blurbs, imagined my own plots, inserted my own twists. In any case the reading of the books was less important than the owning of them. It felt like another act of defiance against Frank.

I bought food too. More and better food. Tinned peaches and glacé cherries, which I ate by the tub, cheese and bread. Alcohol too. I took to drinking red wine by the fireplace.

I bought things and kept on buying things. The internet made it all so easy. I bought things in larger quantities than any single man would ever need. Forty-eight rolls of toilet paper. Two one-kilo cans of instant coffee. Packs of ten five-litre bottles of water. Fifty bars of soap. A year's supply of razor blades (I wasn't prepared to allow Frank's beard to come back). Huge five-kilo sacks of rice, lentils, oats. Industrial quantities of trail mix, prunes and dates. Giant yellow sponges, which you had to cut to size yourself. Bags of cotton wool. Twenty litres of bleach. A 900-litre compost maker. Various adhesives. Electrical tape. Was I preparing for the end of the world? Perhaps this was just what lonely people did?

My days were now filled with work. When I collected the materials from the timber merchants, where

I had not been in months, the conversation was stunted and very awkward. I hated it. When I got back to Lanes End I went immediately down to the rock pools to cool off.

I liked working. I liked the sound my skin made as it brushed along the edges of the mango wood and its sweet smoky scent. I liked the way, if I opened the doors at both ends of the workshop, the air passed through from one door to the other and blew the sawdust onto the ground and the sweat from my forehead. I liked the way the sawdust swirled in mad circles in the corners of the workshop where it sometimes gathered and could not escape.

It was of course irrational to think Ruby had somehow prophesised my accident. The only logical conclusion to draw from Ruby's email was not that she was psychic, but simply that she hated me and wished me harm.

When this thought occurred to me I was looking at my reflection in the mirror. I felt a very powerful urge to hurt myself. I opened one of the boxes of razor blades I had recently purchased and held my forearm out over the sink. But as I was standing there I realised it wouldn't go far enough. It would be a cop-out. It would hurt in the moment but then the pain would fade, the wound would heal and I would be compelled to do it all over again. I needed a form of lasting pain, pain for which there was no treatment. So I began by asking myself an innocuous question: *I wonder what Victoria is doing right now?* I needed, suddenly, to know. It was easy to find out.

I still had a dormant Facebook account that she had created for me years ago. Once I reset the password I was back in, with full access to everyone's public lives. I typed her name into the search bar and clicked into her profile. I scrolled down her page a little. There was a link to Scott's YouTube channel. I clicked through and experienced a feeling similar to when I'm dreaming and in the dream I'm dead but no one is talking about it, as though I've been erased from history, as though I never existed. *Live Well with Scott and Vic.* Beneath this: a picture of the two of them back to back in workout gear, the words *Live Well* printed across their vests. Vic's head is tilted backwards into the nook of his neck. I watched all of the videos. Every last second of every last clip. It was intoxicating, exhilarating: like poking a finger into a festering wound and seeing how deep I could burrow it, how long I could hold it there without passing out.

There was one video I kept coming back to. It was the only one I could find that featured Victoria by herself. In it she is demonstrating various beginner yoga poses. She wears an orange *Live Well* branded singlet top and stretches out on a black yoga mat. She smiles serenely and talks in a low soothing voice that I don't recognise. She reminds me to breathe. She tells me to centre myself, to focus my energy. I watched her movements closely. I sucked air deep down into my body. I played this video over and over. *Don't forget to breathe*, she says.

With Victoria's guidance I began to practice basic yoga on the grass near the garage. I enjoyed closing my eyes and squeezing the grass between my fingers and pushing my chin up to the sky and feeling the skin on my stomach stretch and go taut like a sail and hearing her voice mingle with the sound of the leaves rustling in the wind. The yoga was good for the knee. I could move around much better now but it still throbbed occasionally. This pain, which was only an echo of the original pain, served as a reminder of the precariousness of my isolated situation. What if something bad happened here? I could have an accident in the workshop. Or what if one night the dark figures watching me from the trees came knocking? Who would know? Who would come to help me?

September came. I found the courage to start reading again, beginning with a book I already knew: *Nineteen Eighty-Four*. The daytime was my domain. Whatever was out there in the woods didn't threaten me in the day. I took advantage of this whenever I could. I'd take my book and sit with my bare feet dangling over the edge of the cliff and watch the flat-bottomed clouds drift like giant snails across the peaks on the other side of Wilder Bay. There wasn't a single day of rain that September, and the sun stuck around far longer than it usually does. Usually, I saw squirrels and mice and occasionally skulking foxes and many birds, but that month there was just me and Alfred. Sometimes the silence was so thick it felt like the kind of silence that exists when you hide in a cupboard and hold your breath. The silence of someone wanting not to be found. Once or twice I stood in the centre of the criss-crossing corridors and said *Hello?* and was relieved not to receive any response. I still slept poorly. I spent a lot of time looking at myself in the mirror, inspecting my skin closely for signs of the beard. I bought a magnifying mirror, which made this far easier to do. Upon any sign of stubble I'd whip out the razor blade and scrape it straight off, dry. My face stung a lot because of this rough treatment, but I regarded the pain, the burn, as penance.

I made sure always to get inside before the sun went down. On the nights that I hadn't drunk any wine and therefore wasn't able to sleep, I stood at the window and watched the trees. I was sleeping only three or four hours per night. When I did manage to get some sleep I dreamt a lot. Many of my dreams were simply blank, as though my tired brain hadn't the energy to produce imagery. But there was also a constant whirring and buzzing, an undulating chorus of some sort of diabolical machinery. Gradually, though, I realised it to be the sound of a motorcycle, two motorcycles, revving and groaning, doughnutting all over the muddied landscape of my mind. I remembered with a start one day that this sound had also come to me when I lay semi-conscious in the reeds. Where had this preoccupation with motorcycles come from? This was a mystery that would go unsolved for some weeks.

***

Robbie's life story continues. This doesn't occur every day. Most of the time we're silent. But his past lingers just beneath the surface and the slightest thing sets him off. Invariably, it is something he sees on the telly. He sits forward on my bed so that his feet touch the ground and he stares off into the past and without introduction or warning he reports his visions to me.

I used to think Robbie was a bit of a sad case. I used to pity him. What hubris. We're the same, he and I. Look at us: two lonely, ageing men running the rule over our lives, reliving each painful moment. My motivation for doing so is clear, I hope, at least to you. But Robbie. He seems simply to be flagellating himself to no end. He doesn't have a Lucy Blu-tacked to his wall. It's hard to watch. But also compelling in a darkly entertaining way, knowing, as I already do, half of how his story ends. I'd be lying if I said I wasn't intrigued to know the details of how his life has turned out this way. *Why now?* I asked him when he fell silent again. *What dya mean?* he said. *Why are you going through all of this now? Is something the matter with you? Are you dying?* This was intended as levity. He just sat back on the bed and resumed watching the telly.

***

It was the night before October.

I drank what would be enough, normally, to induce sleep. But something kept me awake. I was frightened. Silly as this sounds – given I had been there by myself for three and a bit months – I was frightened of being there by myself, of my loneliness growing too big and heavy to cast off. Becoming the sort of loneliness which transforms every room into an inescapable cave, every voice into a snub, and every minute into an hour.

The end of summer felt like a bereavement. I toasted the sun. Tomorrow it would leave me, I sensed. The sun had been my companion, in a way my guide and my clock. I was minded of the way I felt after my mother's wake. That night I had written to Ruby for the first time. And miraculously she wrote back. And what a mess I'd made of all that.

In the night I woke with a full bladder. I heard Alfred

fluttering and somewhere the sound of shells scratching across the wooden floor. I saw a streak of light move across the ceiling. I heard an engine. I felt sick and dizzy. I stumbled to the toilet, drank from the tap, went back to bed.

The next morning, October the first, I went up the lane to get the milk and eggs. The anti-fracking sign had been stood back up. Must've been Gray, I thought. The gate was open too. I pushed it shut and heard the latch engage with a clack.

It was too cool now for yoga so in the afternoon I poured myself a glass of wine and read by the fire. I read slowly until a knock at the door disturbed me.

I was surprised to find that I was on my feet. I didn't remember standing up. The chair was still rocking slightly. I held the book at my side and stared in the direction of the door. The fire crackled. I flinched. I didn't want to make a sound. Had I imagined it? … There it was again! Three loud knocks this time. Not in my imagination. Should I answer it? Should I go to the door and call out *Who's there?* I put out the fire and stood pressed against the mantelpiece, eye to eye with Diana. I slowed my breaths and waited. Then I heard the crunch of footsteps out on the shale. They stopped at the window to the left of the fireplace. I stayed as still as a dead thing. The grandfather clock marked off each painful second. Was it slowing down? The footsteps moved off again – crunch, crunch – along the rear wall of the cottage behind the chimney. They moved to the next window over and stopped. Then, after a moment, they moved off again. I crept into the bedroom on all fours and sat on the ground with my back to the bay window, out of sight. My chest was heaving painfully. *Don't forget to breathe.* Who was out there? Constance's lover? The motorcyclists of my dreams? Or, could it be …? Suddenly, my heart leapt, and filled my body with urgent energy. *Victoria! She's here!* So I stood up, on wobbly legs, and marched to the side door. I threw open the door and crunched out onto the shale.

There was a car parked outside on the shale. A red Mini. Maroon in the dusk. Victoria couldn't drive. Who had brought her to me? I approached the car and peered inside. A disc stuck out of the CD player. Tucked into the driver's side door was a little dark book. An atlas? A safety manual? Or something else? This didn't look like a car Victoria had ridden in. Where was the phone charger, for one thing? Where was the two-litre bottle of spring water? Crunching footsteps, somewhere behind me, slowed and then stopped. My throat tightened. If I spoke I would've stammered. I had felt this fear before, I knew it. Standing before my mother's bedroom door, hearing those animal noises coming from within, sensing that something bad was happening on the other side.

'You're reading again.' This was not a voice I knew. I turned, slowly, to face it. There, in the space between the cottage and the workshop, a woman stood before me. Short in stature. Compact. She seemed familiar to me in the way strangers sometimes are, and I stared into her face trying to wring from my brain a droplet of recognition.

'What?'

'In your hand. It's a book.' I looked down at the novel in my hand. I hadn't realised I was still carrying it.

'Oh. Yes.'

'What is it?'

'*Nineteen Eighty-Four*. I'm sorry, who are you?' The woman took a couple of steps toward me and stopped. I stared deep into her features. It was difficult in the half-light to see anything. She took another step and stopped. Only a few metres separated us now. She was poised, standing slightly forward on her toes, in the manner of a runner awaiting the starting gun. I could hear the tide, like a great pot boiling, beyond the trees. Suddenly, I knew who this was.

And I knew why she had come.

I saw now that she held an object in her right hand. Something long, about the size of a rolling pin. I thought about turning to run but I wouldn't have got far across the shale barefoot and with the knee.

'Ruby,' I said.

'Hello, Dan.' There wasn't time to process my thoughts, to sort them into any kind of order. She approached me now. My legs froze. I put a hand onto the roof of the Mini beside me, bracing myself for whatever blows were about to come. She transferred the object from one hand to another. She was standing within easy reach of me. She looked down at the thing in her hand. 'I came here to give you this.' She held it out in front of her and began then to open it out. It was not, I realised, a weapon; it was a roll of paper. 'It's you,' she said. 'Well it's *supposed* to be you.'

I looked at it suspiciously. 'You don't like it,' she said, rolling it back up.

I cleared my throat and said, 'No, I do. It's good.'

'It's yours.' She offered it to me again and I took it. She thrust her hands into her pockets and we stood for a time in silence.

'You're out,' I said.

'Yes. A free woman for nearly a week now.'

'And you came to see me?'

'Well of course I did.'

'But how –'

'– did I find you? Easy really. It just took a little bit of googling. The place names may have been censored but there was enough detail in your letters to figure out where you lived. Wilder-on-Sea; interesting place. There aren't too many remote woodland cottages in Wilder-on-Sea. I actually drove by last night but it was far too late to knock, and I had to be in Stoke this morning to see my Offender Manager, so I went back. Can I use your toilet?'

'Yes, of course,' I said. I led her through the open side door.

'It's kind of weird to be here. I mean, it's like visiting a place in a novel you've read.'

'The toilet is in there.'

'Thank you. Oh, this is nice, very tastefully done, Dan.' She went in and latched the door. I was alone in the corridor. I could easily have slipped away into the trees where I could use my knowledge of the terrain to lose her. But I did not. Something stopped me. When she came out of the toilet I was standing in the open doorway staring out across the shale. 'Oh, you were standing right here the whole time. Could've been embarrassing. Are we going to have a cup of tea then?'

I led Ruby through the criss-crossing corridors into the living room where the doused fire still smouldered. She walked over to the books lining the mantelpiece. I continued on to the kitchen. I paused at the door to ask, 'How do you like it?'

'Sorry?'

'Your tea.'

'Oh, black please. They only gave us powdered milk so I've trained myself to like it black. Oh, and three sugars.' I understood 'they' to mean prison. It was hard to reconcile this person running her finger gently along the spines of my books with the dangerous criminal she apparently was. Almost impossible. I filled the kettle and placed it on the lit stovetop. I opened the kitchen drawer for a teaspoon. Here was a choice, I understood lucidly even in that moment, between trust and death; teaspoon or kitchen knife. I stared at the blade while the kettle began to rattle. I heard Ruby call out something from the living room but I couldn't hear her.

'What?' I shouted. She called again but the kettle was starting to whistle; soon it would be screaming. 'Sorry, I couldn't hear you,' I said as I went through to the living room with two full mugs of tea.

'I was just saying how wonderful it is that you're reading all these books like you said you wanted to.' I put the mugs down on the table between the armchairs.

'I haven't read any of them yet. Only this one,' I said, indicating *Nineteen Eighty-Four*.

'God, I'm so embarrassed about all that Julia and Winston stuff I wrote.' Now I was remembering the sweet words and the haikus and the shared secrets. She sat in the rocking chair. I gave her the black tea. 'Thank you,' she said, and placed it on the stone hearth. 'It's just,' she paused, 'everything there is so, suppressed. Externally I mean. My emotions. That's just how you survive. So everything I felt *inside* became sort of concentrated, heightened, like in a melodrama. I suppose I'm trying to say sorry.'

'You're sorry? For what?'

'For putting you in an awkward position. For pressuring you. For confessing my *undying* love for you.' She laughed a little, nervously. She grabbed her tea and blew on it.

'Don't apologise. I think maybe we were both a bit carried away. I was supposed to be the one helping *you*. Not the other way around. *I'm* the one who should be sorry.' I was still standing, I wasn't comfortable enough yet to sit. I crouched in front of the fire and got it going again.

As I worked she said, 'I need to know one thing.' There was a sudden change in her tone. A solemn drop. I squeezed the poker tightly in my hand. 'Why did you vanish like that?' I was crouched at her feet, I realised. I had put myself in a position of vulnerability without consciously intending to. I stopped working the coals and turned to look up at her. I saw her now, properly, for the very first time. The first and only thought that came into my head was: *she is beautiful*, as it had when I saw her picture on the internet. For a few moments, which felt like falling or floating, I thought this over and over. While I stared silently into her face it may have seemed to her that I was searching for some excuse, inventing a plausible reason for my betrayal, but I wasn't. I was simply tracing the contours of her chin, her cheeks, her eyelids that seemed to swell and contract in the light of the flames, which were flickering slowly into life. I rose and picked up my tea, to buy some thinking time. I had to snap out of this. I didn't really know her at all, or what she might be capable of. Something she wrote in one of her letters suddenly came back to me, about how she became too attached to her patients, that if they didn't turn up to her clinic she'd sometimes visit them demanding to know why. I had to choose my next words carefully.

'I just couldn't write to you any more,' I began, intending in that moment to tell her the truth: that all I had wanted was to save my relationship, that my feelings for her were confusing me, clouding my judgement. But she looked at me with such fierce hope in her eyes that it suddenly seemed impossible. And so I lied. 'I wanted to. I intended to. I got your message, the one about ... love' – saying the word made us both look down into our mugs – 'and I was going to reply to you. It was so nice what you said. I didn't want to rush it. But then, well, things with Vic got ... worse, and everything sort of went out the window. And then I moved here, alone as you've probably already gathered, and she took everything. And I do mean everything. I'm sorry.' Ruby nodded her head continuously as I spoke. I saw in her expression that she wanted to believe this. I knew what

I said had confirmed some optimistic theory in her head about me. She smiled and it was like waiting all the cold night for the dawn and it finally breaking. 'But I remember what you said, about how I was making a mistake. Well, you were right.'

'And with her personal trainer,' Ruby said in the manner of a disapproving gossip, 'what a fucking cliché. I'm sorry, excuse my French.'

'No it's fine. You're right.'

'So, you didn't see any messages from me *after* that one?' she asked sheepishly.

'No,' I lied, 'I don't have internet here. It's actually been liberating. Why? Were there more?'

'Yes. One or two.'

'Oh Ruby, I'm so sorry. You must've thought I'd …' I was surprised at how easily this performance came to me.

'It's probably just as well you didn't get them. Anyway, none of that matters now. I'm free,' she said, shaking her head as if to rid herself of some tiny invisible devil that clung to her hair, 'and so are you.'

'I suppose I am.' There followed a moment of heavy silence. You could feel the air buckling under the weight of the past. We were both so wounded.

'Here's to our freedom,' Ruby said suddenly, boisterously. 'Charge your mugs!' I smiled and raised my mug but I felt gloomy and tense.

'To freedom,' I said and we drank our tea. I lowered myself into an armchair. We sat opposite one another and quietly sipped our tea, both of us looking into the fire. I stole secret looks at her over the brim of my mug.

'Can I ask you a question?' I asked after an interlude.

'Of course.'

'I thought your sentence was seven years. How come you're out now?'

'Depending on the offence you generally only serve half your sentence behind bars. Less in some cases. The other half you serve outside, on licence. So you're free but technically still under Her Majesty's care so there are conditions. One of which is that I have to attend weekly meetings with my Offender Manager back in Stoke, which is where I was this morning.'

'What happens if you miss a meeting?'

'There'd be a hearing. My offence was violent, so they'd probably send me straight back.' She was remarkably open and matter-of-fact about all of this. I got no sense from her body language or tone that she was suppressing any kind of resentment towards me. But still, it wasn't clever to trust her so quickly.

'So, and I hope you don't mind me asking about this.'

'No, go ahead,' she said, settling back in the rocking chair.

'Is how you described the … incident to me exactly how it happened?'

'You mean Lee's accident?' There was something sinister in her choice of the word *accident*. Perhaps I'd been reading too much Orwell. But it sharpened me like a scrape on a whetstone. I nodded. She began to laugh. 'Look at me. I'm five-three. You think I could throw an angry fifteen-stone man down the stairs?' She rose then from the rocking chair and looked around the room. 'It's so traditional here,' she said, steering the conversation into cooler territory. 'Look at that clock. It's beautiful. Everything looks so, I don't know, *old*.' I had to hand it to her. If she was pretending it didn't show. 'It's kind of how I pictured it, this place, when you were describing it to me. You've done precisely what you set out to. You've made a home. You should be proud of yourself.'

'I don't know about that.'

We fell silent again. She walked to the window, left of the fireplace.

'Do you mind that I came?' She pulled aside the net curtain and peered out at the swaying pines.

'Of course not. I mean, it *is* a bit of a shock to see you in real life. But I'm glad you're here. You're right, though, it's like meeting a character from a novel.'

'But one you remember fondly.'

'You look different.' I flushed with heat. I'd misstepped.

'I do? Compared to what? I never sent you any pictures.'

'I may have googled you.'

'Oh. Fair enough I suppose. I had to google this place to find you. I'm curious, where did you see me? What did I look like?'

'There was a write-up in a local paper. In the photo they used you were outside. Your face is the same but there's something different that I can't put my finger on.' Ruby leant her weight on the windowsill and smiled.

'It must be my hair. It's red now. Ruby red. I got Jade to colour it for me. It was practically the first thing we did after I got out. I wanted a change. I needed *colour*.'

'So you're staying with her?'

'Yes. She has a house in Staffordshire, in the countryside. Well, I say countryside but it's nothing like as remote as this. She has neighbours for a start.'

What are we doing here? I thought. What is this? All the things we talked about in our letters swelled before us like a restless sea and here we were tramping about in puddles of small talk. 'Out of curiosity, how did you know Victoria wouldn't be here?' I didn't believe for a second she'd come just to give me the portrait.

'I didn't. But I'd have been surprised if she was. Things sounded pretty desperate in your letters. I'm sorry about your mother, by the way. I know that's super late but I just wanted to say it in person.'

'Thank you.'

Could this woman love me? Could it all have been true? I ached to know what went through her head.

'My father died a couple of months ago.'

'Oh, I'm sorry.'

'He left Jade the house. I was written out, of course. Disowned. The rest of his estate went to Camila, his Spanish wife. She's younger than me. They thought he'd drowned because he was found face down in the jacuzzi but it was a heart attack.' She looked out at the pines again.

I felt a surge of pity and then, immediately after, a stab of anxiety. Why was she looking into the darkness? Was there someone out there, someone she was waiting for?

'Is it strange to be out?'

'The only strange thing is that nothing has changed. Three and a half years feels like three hundred years when you're inside. But everything's just the same. And worse. I'm disappointed.'

'What will you do?'

'You mean with the rest of my life? I don't know. I can't practise psychotherapy any more. Jade suggested travel. She's offered to sell the house and give me half. I've always wanted to travel.'

'Where would you go?'

'Somewhere green. Maybe India. I've always wanted

to see the Taj Mahal, to see the bench where Diana sat in her red jacket. I'm not sure. Travelling feels like running away. I suppose that's literally what it is.' She paused for thought. 'But I wanted to see you. I knew *that*. So I just did it. I came. And it feels good to see you, Dan. Perhaps that's what I should do, just follow my instincts. When we ignore our instincts, that's when we get into trouble.'

'I think you're right about that,' I said, and I truly meant it. Ruby finished her tea and placed it on the hearth. She did not sit back down. She looked at me and smiled weakly. Were there, too, things she wanted to say but couldn't?

Abruptly, she stood up straight as though to announce her departure. 'Well, thanks for the tea.'

'Of course,' I said and rose too.

Now that she was leaving, I felt a strange sense of loss. I seemed not to mean very much to her after all. Not nearly as much as I'd thought. I wasn't this great lost love that she needed to exorcise. I wasn't an enemy to be destroyed. *I'm disappointed*, she said, and whether or not she was referring to me didn't matter, because in my head she meant me.

I walked her outside. It was late now. Fully dark. I sensed a strange and exciting opportunity was passing me by. She wound down the passenger-side window.

'It was so lovely to see you, Dan'. She turned the key in the ignition. The engine coughed dryly. She tried it again. I knew instantly what the problem was, I could hear it. No fuel. She tried a third time. 'Shit.'

'Look at your petrol gauge.'

'FUCK!' Ruby looked over at the Transporter parked beside her on the shale. 'Do you have any spare fuel, just to get me to the petrol station?'

'Van's diesel.'

'Right.'

'Why don't you stay the night?' The words just came out of me. 'There's plenty of room; you'd have a bed. We can get petrol and set you on your way in the morning.'

Was it fear of loneliness that pushed me into making this impulsive offer? Or something else?

'Are you sure? I passed a pub up the road that probably has rooms.' But I could tell she didn't really mean it; she sounded relieved.

'Of course. You've come all this way, it's the least I can do.' Ruby mulled this over. She pulled the key from the ignition and got out of the Mini.

'Thank you, Dan,' she said with sincerity. 'I guess I didn't factor in the petrol I would use looking for this place. It's quite well hidden, you know? I was driving around for ages. I only found it after I was given directions.'

'Someone gave you directions?'

'Yes, a farmer up the way. I think his name was Gray.

At first when I saw his place I thought: *this must be it*, so I pulled up. I was relieved to hear him say he wasn't you after I met him. He was drunk. And the place was a state. Couple of pit bulls chained up barking like mad and two sad-looking teenagers sitting on a bale of hay smoking. Very welcoming. I suppose they were his sons. Still he told me how to find your place.'

'Were you by any chance the one who stood the fracking sign back up?'

'Oh yes that was me. Sorry. Bit of a neat freak. We can go and knock it back down in the morning if you want?' I watched her grab a handbag from under the driver's seat, which I hadn't seen earlier, and slip the little dark book from the door compartment inside it. 'Thank you so much. I'm sorry for the trouble.' She closed the driver's door sharply and locked the Mini.

Standing in the corridor outside the box room – where I had made up the bed – I presented Ruby with a tooth-brush and a clean towel. It was clear we both felt drained, and though it was still only ten o'clock it felt later.

'Help yourself to anything you want in the kitchen.'

'Thanks. I'm an early riser, though – I hope that won't bother you.'

'No, I'm the same.'

'Oh good,' she said and hugged the towel to her belly.

'Well, goodnight then,' I said.

'Goodnight.' I walked away and heard the box room door squeak on its hinges but it did not click shut. I turned around. 'I don't cope well with enclosed spaces these days,' she said.

'Right of course. I'm sorry, that room is so small.'

'No, it's fine really if I leave the door ajar.'

'OK, well. Just knock on my door if you need anything.'

'Will do.'

I went into my bedroom and stood at the closed door for a while listening for movement on the other side. It was silent. Eventually, I heard the *ka-dunk* of the pull cord in the box room and knew she'd switched the light off.

It was surreal to think of Ruby lying just a matter of metres away from me. It was like I had conjured her into existence. She'd walked straight from the virtual world into my life, passing by Victoria as she made the opposite journey. Victoria was now the one who existed only on a screen. I walked to the window and looked up to see a fat bright moon. Despite being exhausted I knew I wouldn't sleep easily so I stayed at the window and scanned the trees. But was I stupid to think the threat was outside? Maybe it was already here, three paces down the corridor.

At around one in the morning a terrible thought

occurred to me. The laptop! It was on clear display through the window of the workshop. Ruby would only need to see that to realise I'd lied to her. I had to do something with it before the morning. I snuck out of my room, stole silently along the corridor to the door and tiptoed as lightly as I could across the shale. The laptop's little green lights blinked at the far end of the workshop. When I pressed the spacebar to wake it up, the screen bathed the workshop in blue light. This was a risk, I knew. Ruby might be a bad sleeper too, she could've wandered out at any moment. The video was still paused. Victoria's mouth was open, baring her newly perfect teeth. I stared at it with shame, with longing. I watched the video for about thirty seconds before pausing it. Then I pulled the Chinese folding screen over from the corner where it stood next to little Daniel's dismantled cot and arranged it so that it shielded the laptop. I just had to hope Ruby hadn't already seen it. Then I left the workshop, locking it behind me, and went back inside the cottage. I tried to close the door behind me as delicately as I could but it still made a noise. I winced and waited but there was no movement from inside the box room. I climbed into bed, sure that I would now be able to sleep – but not before I had wedged a chair under the door handle.

I woke to a scream. Then, a crashing sound like a pile of

things falling over. I looked at the Nokia. Three forty-two. I jumped out of bed, grabbed the claw hammer, which I had recently taken to keeping in my bedside drawers, then pulled the chair away from the door and dashed into the corridor. I opened the door to the box room and switched the light on. Ruby was standing on the bed waving her arms wildly above her head. Her hair, which she'd said was ruby red but was actually a deeper plum colour, covered her face in a chaotic swirl. The plastic storage cartons had been toppled over and Constance Lovett's things were spilled across the floor. Ruby ran past me into the corridor emitting a high-pitched sound. Not fully in control of myself I ran into the box room with the hammer primed by my ear. My arms and legs were throbbing with adrenaline. I looked down and saw Alfred perched on the rail at the head of the bed. I exhaled deeply and lowered the hammer. Ruby was whimpering in the corridor behind me.

'I see you've met Alfred.'

'What?' Ruby said, wafting her hands violently through her hair.

'It's all right, there's nothing there,' I said, taking her wrists and calming her.

'In the room. There's something ...'

'... Yes, that's Alfred. He lives here. He goes where he wants.' Ruby leant out from behind me to peek into the box room. She saw him. Alfred buried his orange beak in his green feathers and started rummaging. He seemed oblivious to the carnage around him. Or indifferent.

'Wow. He's beautiful.'

'He's a quaker parrot.'

'A quaker?'

'Yes. Or a monk parakeet.'

'Look at the colour of him.' She freed her wrists from my grip now, which I noticed she had not objected to, and crept into the room. 'Look at you,' she said to Alfred, approaching him slowly, 'aren't you pretty?' I watched her tiptoe to the bed. She didn't seem self-conscious in my company clad only in a singlet top and underpants. 'You go where you want to, hey? So you're free too?' She crawled across the bed towards him and he jumped down from the rail to greet her. Memories of Victoria on her knees in the back room at Beryl Avenue waving the little stick in circles about his and Oscar's heads came flooding back. 'I'm sorry, Dan,' she turned to look at me. 'I didn't mean to scream like that.' Alfred took off now and fluttered into the nursery.

'No, I'm sorry. I should've told you about him. It slipped my mind.'

'He just gave me a fright. I heard something sort of scurrying about and I thought it could be anything out here in the countryside, maybe a rat. And then I felt something on my face.'

'I feel terrible.'

'Don't. Please. It's no big deal.' I went into the box room and began putting the mess into some kind of order. Some plates had smashed. It would be no good trying to sort through this stuff properly now so I simply pushed everything into a less messy pile away from the bed. As I was doing this I spotted Ruby's handbag on its side. Her belongings had spilled out across the floor. Tissues, a pack of menthol cigarettes, a lighter, lipstick, a hairbrush, keys with a Mini keyring, another set of keys, an old Nokia like mine and … the little dark book. Her purse had fallen out too and I saw something poking out from it that made my heart jump. It was a driver's licence. But it wasn't hers. It was her sister's. Why would Ruby have Jade's licence? I remembered then that they were identical twins.

I looked up at her now. 'Now at least you won't cut your feet on the china.'

'Thank you. You're very thoughtful.'

I rose then to leave her. 'Well, goodnight take two I guess.'

'Goodnight Dan.' I went to close the door. 'Can you leave it ajar please?'

'Oh, right, yes, of course.'

'I'm just not used to pitch dark.'

I went back into my bedroom and replaced the chair beneath the door handle. Before I put the claw hammer back in its drawer I turned it over in my hand. I had surprised myself in the box room. I had been ready and quite willing to use it.

The next morning, after a dreadful sleep, I got up at six. The door to her room was still ajar. I didn't dare peer inside.

In the living room our mugs were still there, Ruby's on the hearth, mine on the small table. I noticed a gap in the row of books. Had she taken one? I hadn't heard anything in the night; she must've moved like a spirit. I took the mugs into the kitchen and filled the kettle with water. I spotted my portrait on the table. I rolled it out flat. There was something eerie about it. It just wasn't me but there was an uncanniness about it that tickled like an ant on the back of my neck. I recognised things about the man, little details: the mole on his cheek, the pinkness of his lower eyelids, the wispiness of his hair. The kettle began to whistle. I made coffee. Then I realised that it looked just like my father.

'That smells good.' I heard Ruby's voice behind me. I turned around. She was standing with one leg in front of the other in the doorway as though paused mid stride. She was barefoot and still wearing only the singlet. I wasn't sure where to put my eyes.

'Good morning. There's plenty of water. I'll grab another mug.'

'I couldn't sleep so I borrowed this,' she brandished a book: *Wuthering Heights*, 'I hope you don't mind?'

'Of course not. Someone ought to read them.'

'I was wondering which one to take, you have so many good ones, but being here, in this place, just lent itself so well to this one.'

'My father loved *Wuthering Heights*.'

'Then he had great taste.'

I gave Ruby her coffee. I sat down and began to drink mine.

'Oh god, the painting. Look at it!' Ruby stood at the foot of the table, taking in the length of the portrait. 'It's nothing like you at all is it?'

'Not really. But it does look just like my father.'

'You're kidding?'

'Somehow you've painted a freakishly accurate portrait of my father. He even had a mole on his cheek right there like that.' She pulled a chair up and sat nearer to it, nearer to me.

'That *is* freaky! Will you hang it? You don't have to.'

'Of course I will.'

Ruby beamed. I remembered what she said, in one of her letters, about doing somersaults into her father's pool trying to impress him, trying to get his attention. We sat in silence then, sipping our coffees and poring over the painting. The October sky was the colour of faded slate. Through the open window we could hear the pines rubbing against each other in the wind.

'Before we go to get the fuel, how about you give me

a guided tour? I feel part of this place. I read all of your work logs remember?'

'They weren't work logs.'

'You went into a *lot* of detail, Dan. *Yesterday I shaved the edge of a door with my edge-shaving implement. Today I painted a wall shocking pink.*'

'There are no pink walls in this house.'

'Prove it.'

After coffee we washed and dressed and I took her around the cottage. Then we went outside. I walked her over to the workshop and she peered through the glass. The laptop was perfectly hidden behind the Chinese screen. She asked me what I was working on. I said nothing in particular and shepherded her to the end of the driveway, where I intended to walk her through the woods to the rock pools. I was almost to the trees when I heard the steel garage door screeching open behind me.

'That's just an empty garage,' I said, running over and positioning myself in her way. 'I don't use it.'

The router was in there. If she saw it …

'I like empty places,' Ruby said and bumped me playfully to one side and began tugging again at the door.

I thought for a second about creating a distraction, but what?

'Oh, what's this?' She slipped inside through the gap

and emerged a few seconds later holding aloft the Brexit placard. 'Let's take back control, Dan!' She pointed at me with a serious expression on her face and then burst into laughter. 'Why do you have this?'

'It was foisted upon me.'

'So you didn't vote Leave?'

'I didn't vote at all.'

'And you're not against fracking either?'

'I don't even really know what fracking is.'

'Fair enough.' She gave me the placard and marched into the woods. I threw it back into the garage and pulled the door shut. I would have to padlock it.

Signs of her true personality were beginning to emerge. She was spontaneous, impish. But I sensed in her a relentless spirit, a sort of defiant tenacity when there was something, however whimsical, she wanted.

'Come on!' she yelled from the trees.

We proceeded across the soft, pine-carpeted ground with Ruby in front and me behind. When she saw the sea she was energised. She ran to the edge of the cliff and peered down into it as it washed lazily against the rocks.

'Now this is a view,' she said when I caught up with her. She inhaled deeply. 'Since I got out all I've seen is Stoke. This is such a tonic. Is that the Lakes over there?'

I nodded. 'The view's even better when it's clear.'

'I think the view's just fine,' she said solemnly. I

looked at her and I had the sense that this was truly a woman savouring her freedom. I doubted whether her sister could've acted this well. 'Do you mind if we just sit here a bit?'

And so we sat and looked out at the sea.

On the drive to get petrol, Ruby put on the radio and peered out of the window at the country. At the petrol station I filled a jerry can with unleaded, enough to get her back to Stoke, and Ruby went inside to pay. When she climbed back into the Transporter I could sense instantly that the atmosphere had changed. Her energy was gone. I felt flatter too. I didn't immediately start the engine. There seemed to be words rising inside me but they died in my throat, half-formed, and I swallowed them back down. I rolled the Transporter slowly off the forecourt and onto the road.

On the drive back, Ruby did not turn on the radio. The silence between us was the first noticeable one since she'd arrived. I drove as far as the turn-off towards Lanes End and stopped. As the engine idled and I waited for a gap in the invisible traffic Ruby asked if I was hungry.

'Starving,' I said, and swung the Transporter around in a violent U-turn back towards Wilder.

This was the second of October.

I pulled up at a greasy spoon on the seafront and ordered two full Englishes and a pot of tea for two.

'Can I ask you something?' I said.

'Of course,' Ruby was opening the lid of the stainless steel teapot and stirring the teabags around.

'How are you able to pay for things? Like, for instance, the petrol.'

'I'm lucky. I've got Jade to help me out. I don't know what I would've done if I didn't have her. When you're released you're given forty-eight quid and sent on your merry way. What's a woman supposed to do with forty-eight quid?' She closed the teapot lid and inspected the steam rising from her teaspoon. 'Not everyone qualifies for benefits. Plus, even if you do qualify you have to wait twelve weeks to be assessed first. Plus, they only pay direct into bank accounts these days and what if you don't have a bank account, or even a fixed abode to apply for one? Some charities can sort you out with job opportunities before you get out, but that's very rare. I guess if you don't have anywhere to go when you get out you might end up on the streets. A lot of the women I knew inside had reoffended within twenty-four hours of getting out because they felt they had no other choice. Robbing. Selling themselves. Either make some quick cash and eat, maybe get enough for a night in a hostel, or else end up back inside, where they're used to. At least it's warm and dry inside.'

'That's terrible.'

'The whole system is, Dan. There's a lot of good women who could lead good lives if they were given a fair crack. Like I said, I'm lucky, I have family. But a lot of women get stuck in the machine and never get out.' A waitress delivered the fry-ups. We dug in ravenously.

'You must be so relieved to be out.'

Ruby nodded. Her eyes had welled a little.

'Yes,' she said, through a mouthful of food. A bit of toast flew across the table and landed on my sleeve. She laughed and a tear fell from her eye now. I laughed too.

It was a dry day. After breakfast we walked a little along the prom. Anti-fracking signs had been affixed to the suicide prevention fencing on the tidal walls. Bold black capital letters on a yellow background. It looked like we were quarantined, like the whole of Wilder-on-Sea was contaminated, condemned. Beyond the fences the grey western sky was milky over the sea. Ahead of us an old lady in a tabard struggled to pull an A-board into the pavement. It read: PAYDAY LOANS and on the other side: PALMS READ HERE. We tried to peer into the shop window but it was obscured entirely by bits of long silver tinsel. Then the wind picked up and Ruby wasn't dressed for it so we went back to the Transporter.

Back at Lanes End I asked Ruby to open the Mini's petrol cap so I could pour the unleaded petrol in. She gave me the keys and said to do it myself as she had to make a phone call. I opened the driver's side door and pulled the lever to open the petrol cap. I was tempted to have a look in the glove compartment but it was impossible; she was right there in plain view. Once I'd filled up the car, the jerry can was useless to me as I drove a diesel, so I opened the boot of the Mini to put it in. To my surprise there was one already there – and it was filled with petrol. I turned around to look at Ruby: she was walking mindless circles in the middle of the clearing with her Nokia to her ear. She was smirking and giggling, almost coquettishly, in the way women with secrets sometimes did, I thought, recalling Victoria's face whenever she received a text. Who was she talking to? I put the empty jerry can next to the full jerry can and closed the boot.

She was finishing her phone call and looking very pleased with herself as she walked back towards me, a dreamy sort of expression on her face.

'Is everything all right?' I asked.

'Yes. That was Jade. She was expecting me back last night so I thought I'd better check in with her. She knew I was coming to meet you. She thought I was crazy reckless for coming. You might have been a complete nutter.'

There was a long pause as we stood before one another fiddling with our hands.

'I suppose you'll be off then?' I said eventually,

miserably. She nodded and pressed her lips together in a non-smile.

There was so much to doubt about her, so much to fear. So why did I feel so wretched about her leaving? An aeroplane passed overhead. I felt heavy, drained of all energy. She made a move then towards the driver's door.

'I don't want you to go,' I blurted suddenly. 'I mean, I want you to stay. For a bit.'

'A bit?'

'Yes. Or more. If you want.'

'Why?' she said, walking closer to me.

'I'm thinking of redecorating.' I could think of nothing else. 'You could help. You could paint.'

'You want me to stay so I can help paint your house?' I nodded, crossing my arms, trying and failing to conceal the grin that was emerging on my face. 'And just how long do you plan to have me here?'

'I don't know. Until it's finished?' *Or until I figure out who you really are,* I added in my head.

She turned away slowly, making a show of considering my proposition. 'I'll stay. But only because your cottage is so *depressing*.' She marched past me towards the cottage, clearly enjoying herself. I followed her.

'I thought you liked it? You said it was beautiful.'

'I said the *clock* was beautiful. I think the word I used to describe the house was *traditional*. It's just a bit … gloomy. It needs some colour.'

'See, this is why I need you to stay.'

'Oh yes, you need my artistic *vision*, sure. I understand.'

If this all seems terribly impulsive, Lucy, it's because it was. What Ruby had said about following our instincts rang true, and you have to remember where we'd come from, what we'd suffered, respectively. Yes, there was a voice inside telling me to be wary, reminding me of the things about her that didn't add up, but my instinct spoke louder and it was telling me to explore this dangerous attraction that I felt. I know she felt this too because – why else would she have stayed?

Ruby went from room to room scribbling things in a pad that she wouldn't let me see. *Let me work,* she said when I tried to grab it. Later we drove to the big Tesco and bought a rotisserie chicken and a baguette and sat at the kitchen table with a bottle of red wine. We talked about her time inside. We talked about my time alone here. We talked about our mothers. Our fathers. Our childhoods. Our letters. The conversation came so easily and I wondered when I had ever talked so much in my life. It was like a great balloon of words had been pierced within and I could feel them rushing up and out of me. It got dark and we said goodnight in the corridor and this time I went to bed and did not barricade the door.

The next morning she was gone. I had half expected it.

In the kitchen our wine glasses were still out on the side. The outline of her lips was misty in the morning light. I stood for a time in the doorway of the box room staring at the space she'd occupied in the bed. I went in and straightened the sheets. There was nothing of hers left behind. She'd left no trace except for a single red hair on the pillow. I put it in my pocket. The cartons that she'd knocked over two nights before were still in a mess on the floor. I tidied their contents back inside the cartons and reassembled them into a more solid stack. As I worked I spotted something gleaming under the bed. I lay on my belly and stretched to reach it. It was a steak knife. I turned it over in my hand. Had it spilt from one of the cartons, or had Ruby had this in her handbag? It certainly didn't match the rest of Constance's cutlery. It was too modern, too unused. I put it in the kitchen drawer.

All through the cottage a deep quiet reigned. Alfred was listless. We were alone again. In the bathroom I looked intently at my reflection. I had allowed the outline of my chin to darken. How could I have been so negligent? I grabbed my razor and with shaking hands scraped the stubble off immediately. In my haste I cut myself: a perfectly straight laceration an inch long just above my chin on the right side. I watched it bleed. A red shape, like a tattered sail, painted itself on my chin.

I went into the workshop and watched the video of Victoria a few times and then felt very low indeed. And then, almost unbidden, the image of Ruby's sister's driving licence came into my head. And the full jerry can. And the steak knife under her bed. And then I was opening a new tab and frantically googling. I didn't know what I was looking for. I was just following my nose. I remembered that they were identical twins. I brought up Jade's social media pages. *Jade Holland*. Her Facebook page had been used sparingly in the last few years, there was only a handful of very recently uploaded photos. But there were hundreds of photos of her from years before. Christmas pics. Holiday snaps. In one she is standing by a swimming pool somewhere sunny. How she resembled Ruby! And then I looked Ruby up on Facebook too. *Ruby Holland*. Under '*Friends*' only one person: Jade. Only one photo uploaded: of Jade. Caption: 'Twinny!' The account looked brand new. Granted, she'd just come out of prison, but there was something off about it. I began flicking through Jade's photos again. Eventually, I found one of Ruby uploaded a couple of weeks earlier. A selfie. She is wearing a bobble hat and you cannot see her hair. Caption: 'Ruby. My villainous twin.'

I found no photos of them together.

Around half-three, drinking tea at the kitchen table, I

heard the crunching of wheels on the shale and went outside to investigate. It was the Mini.

'This project is going to take time. A girl needs her bits,' she said, padding past me into the cottage, a couple of Tesco carrier bags in each hand. I followed her inside to the box room. 'What happened to your face?'

'Oh,' my hand rose to my chin. 'I cut it shaving.'

'Jesus, be careful.' She set the carrier bags down on the little bed, blew out her cheeks. 'I could murder a brew,' she said, smiling inscrutably.

Later, we drove to B&Q. Ruby threw cans of paint into the trolley with abandon. Yellows, reds, purples, blues, greens. Lots of different shades of green. Two very large vats of white. Brushes of all breadths, all types. Rollers. When we got back to the cottage we put everything down in the corridor and stood back looking at the haul, our hands on our hips.

'I'm going to start in there,' she said, indicating the nursery.

Over the next few days we established a kind of routine. In the morning one of us would fetch the eggs and milk from the gate (we took it in turns), we'd have breakfast in the kitchen (together), shower (separately), then Ruby would work in the nursery and I'd lock myself in the workshop. After a few hours we'd meet in the kitchen for lunch. Mostly we made sandwiches out of whatever was to hand. One time Ruby cooked soup and we ate it with stale bread made good again in the oven. There seemed always to be a bottle of wine open, always a few empties clustered on the work surface. I found her more and more attractive.

Ruby would not let me into the nursery. She hung a sheet in the window so I couldn't peek from the courtyard.

Sometimes Ruby disappeared for an hour or so. I never knew where she went. She said she went for walks – *little wanderings*, she called them – down to the sea, the marshland, to watch the birds and the boats way off in Wilder Bay, or into the woods to listen to the trees. Sometimes at night. It was a 'grounding technique', she said. A way of getting out of her head – away from the dark memories of prison within, about which she never offered any detail – and focusing instead on something in the present, something tangible. A sound, a smell, a texture.

Though I kept the latch on the inside of the workshop door, Ruby never once came knocking while I worked. I respected her *wanderings* and she in turn seemed to respect my workspace. Which was just as well I suppose except this emboldened me to watch Vic's video constantly. Indeed I kept it on its usual loop while I whittled and measured and hammered and sawed, the volume down low. It was a compulsion.

Sometimes I used this private time to do more digging into Ruby's past. I felt guilty doing it but I just couldn't rid myself of the sense that something was off here, a feeling like I had forgotten or misplaced something. I had never spoken to Jade, but I had seen Ruby out on the clearing supposedly on the phone to her many times. Was it really Jade on the phone? Was the real Ruby Holland still behind bars somehow directing the play? Or was I being paranoid? Ever since I first looked up Jade's Facebook page my suspicion had only grown. I found the local newspaper coverage of Ruby's trial and zoomed in on the picture. The caption said: *7 years: Ms Holland*. No first name. How had I missed that? Was it important? I hadn't looked at the picture in all this time. But now that I was looking at it again I sensed I had also seen it somewhere else. I stared at the portrait, at her tired eyes, at her sad smiling mouth. The newspaper credited the photo to Facebook. Frantically, and with an ear to the latched door, I clicked through the dozens and dozens of photos on Jade's Facebook page until I found it. The very same picture. Jade, in the park. Jade, with a man next to her, cropped out by the newspaper. No caption. Date: 2013. Before the prison term. Was this it then? Proof? Of what? That Ruby was lying to me? That she was Jade posing as Ruby? Or simply that a journalist had been lazy, or sloppy, when they lifted the picture? The story was so short, probably a junior's work, and in the absence of any social media presence of Ruby's own, perhaps the reporter simply stole a photo of the identical twin. And who would ever know? Who would ever look closely enough to realise? Who would ever care? But just because there was a possible explanation it didn't mean my first hunch wasn't right. It wasn't yet possible to draw a reliable conclusion. But what I began to grow increasingly certain of was that, one way or another, something strange was happening.

A week passed. It became time for Ruby to travel back to Stoke for her weekly meeting with her Offender Manager. It was early in the morning and the October sun gave off little warmth. Ruby came at me with a tea towel intended as a blindfold. Her cold fingers fluttered against the back of my neck as she tied a knot. She led me by the small of my back into the nursery.

'Are you ready?'

'Yep.'

'OK. Here we go.' She pulled the tea towel from my eyes. This is what I saw. Plants. Tendrils. Leaves. A forest. I looked up at the ceiling: a canopy of trees. I looked down; dense undergrowth of mushrooms and plants and animals. It was alive. And everything green. Yellow-green. Black-green. Blue-green. Red-green. Not a spot of wall or ceiling had been missed by her brush. Violent colour everywhere. A supersaturation of colour.

'Look,' she said, and pointed down at a corner, 'ivy.' She traced her pointed finger over a long meandering snake of ivy leaves. It ran behind things, in front of things, twined around things, across every wall, unbroken. 'I want there to be ivy running through the entire house. I want it everywhere.' The back of my throat began to harden.

'Thank you,' I said. 'Thank you so much. It's ...' I could not articulate myself.

'It was my pleasure.' She rubbed gentle circles into my back.

I watched the red Mini disappear around the bend into the woods and instantly I felt loneliness creep forward to the edge of the trees, its nostrils flaring. I went back inside the cottage and did not come out again, not to work, not to watch the video, not for anything.

I needed to occupy myself, my hands, my thoughts. So I went through the cottage tidying, cleaning. Ruby was messy, and quite content to let me straighten things up after her. I smiled at the little piles of female paraphernalia which I had once been so familiar with, that had begun to amass in little clusters in the box room, the bathroom. Tissues, cotton buds, bobbles. Tubes and pots of cream, lotion and serum the use for all of which men can only guess at. I found a few hairclips lying on the bathroom floor and dropped them into the top drawer of the bedside table in the box room. Something within caught my eye. A box of tablets. I picked it up. There was a sticker on the side.

SEROQUEL TABS 400mg.
Take with or just after food. Warning: read the additional information given with this medicine.

I looked inside. There were no tablets left. I put the box in my pocket.

That night, now I was alone again, the old fears returned. Lanes End was once again a house of terrors. I tried to pick up *Nineteen Eighty-Four* again but it was a mistake. I drank but it wasn't the same alone. I fidgeted and tidied and stood in the nursery for a long time running my gaze over every miraculous detail of Ruby's mural. The weather was cold now and getting colder each day. I wrapped myself in a blanket and sat on the bed in the box room and read and reread the page in *Wuthering Heights* that Ruby had saved with a fold; the scene where Heathcliff hangs the dog. I fell asleep there.

The next morning I went into the workshop with the empty box of tablets and googled Seroquel. It was an anti-psychosis medication. In smaller doses, up to 400mg per day, they were prescribed as antidepressants, used to manage symptoms of anxiety, depression and bipolar disorder. But in larger daily doses, up to 800mg, they were used to manage symptoms of mania and schizophrenia. I looked down at the empty box next to the laptop. These tablets were 400mg each. How many she had been taking each day I had no way of knowing. I rummaged my fingers inside the box, hoping to find an information slip, a prescription, an advisory note, anything that might shed some light. But there were just the two empty tablet trays. I felt nervous jitters taking hold and needed to find something to do. So I closed the laptop, put the empty Seroquel box in a drawer and set about hanging Ruby's painting. I found a deep, three-tiered well frame, walnut, among the antiques and hung my father's portrait in the sitting room above the fire, above his books. Now he and Diana ruled the room together.

The rest of the day I worked on the trunks. When the sun went down I scurried across the shale into the cottage and locked the door behind me. Ruby had awakened something within me that was good, but clearly she'd stirred another part of me too. When I looked at her I didn't know who I was seeing.

A few days earlier I had posed as a reporter and written to Inbox Inmate and asked what their policy was when it came to protecting the identity of inmates. That is, did inmates have to use fake names or were they obligated to use their own? Their response gave me no peace. Inmates were protected by the same laws as those on the outside, it said. That is, they might use a pseudonym if they chose or their real name. Exasperated, I broke cover and called their telephone support line from my Nokia, cupping my mouth so the sound wouldn't travel, to ask specifically about the supposedly recently released *Ruby Holland* and was politely informed that the Data Protection Act 1998 precluded the sharing of that information.

That night I dreamt again of motorcycles. Again just the sound. No accompanying imagery. No devils, no monsters, no trapdoors. Just the sound of motorcycle engines distantly revving. In the morning I pulled back the curtains and peered up at the sky. It was cloudy and threatening rain. Ominous weather. But nothing had befallen me in the night. No one had come for me. Not Ruby. Not even Jade.

When I went to get the eggs and milk something out on the clearing caught my eye. I walked across the grass towards it. The clearing was soft and marshy underfoot. The thing was an empty milk bottle. It was just lying there on its side in the middle of the clearing. Holding it in my hand I looked up and saw now that the shed door was open. As I squelched over to it I wondered how I'd slept through a storm strong enough to force it open. I went to close it but noticed that there was a great puddle of milk on the ground inside. Painted violently across the back wall a dozen yellow splodges; the exploded yolks of twelve eggs. Orange-yellow tendrils had oozed down the wall and mingled with the milk (far too much to have come from just one bottle) and woodchip mulch on the ground. Shards of broken glass bobbed like tiny icebergs in the obscene mixture. I dropped the empty bottle on the ground and ran back across the clearing. I slipped on a slick bit of ground. I stopped and looked down and saw a tyre mark in the grass. It was unmistakably a motorcycle's. I ran for the cottage, bolts of pain zapping up my body from my bad knee, and into the kitchen. I downed a glass of water and closed my eyes, feeling the cold morning air move fast and rough through my chest. Alfred came fluttering in as though sensing my distress and perched on the windowsill. Did this mean I hadn't imagined the motorcycle engines? Were they actually out there, riding by night across the countryside?

Ruby pulled up in the Mini just before sunset. The light was rapidly fading and the trees were losing their colour and individuality, becoming a black spiky mass. I went out to meet her. She turned off the engine and fidgeted a while with something on her lap. As I watched her I began to feel anxious. She'd been away longer than I anticipated and I couldn't help feeling suspicious about the timing of her return – was it too convenient that she'd been absent the night of the shed incident?

She rose from the car smiling. I'd forgotten how

small she was. Her hair was tied back and she wore tight blue jeans and a red leather jacket. She retrieved a bag from the boot. I wondered, when she saw that I'd put the empty jerry can in there, whether she'd realised that I knew she'd manipulated me into letting her stay in the cottage.

'Hi! Sorry, I was just texting Jade to let her know I'd arrived safe.'

'Hi.' I looked into her eyes.

'Hi,' she said again, more softly this time, and meeting my gaze intently. We stood like this for a few moments, just looking at each other and smiling.

'Glad you're back.'

'Me too.'

'Thought maybe you weren't coming back.'

'I stayed an extra night at home. Jade wanted to spend some time. I only realised when it was too late that I didn't have your number. Otherwise I would've texted.'

'Let me take that,' I said reaching for her bag.

But she wouldn't let go of it. Her grip on it was tight. Her knuckles were white. 'It's alright, I've got it.'

'How is Jade?'

'Shall we go in?' she said, hunching her shoulders and stepping from one foot to the other. Was she avoiding the question? 'It's a bit fresh.'

A few moments later we were in the sitting room drinking wine. Ruby was stood before the mantelpiece.

'I can't believe how good it looks up there.' She meant the painting. 'It was on the wall of my cell for so long, above my bed. And now it's here, in this place. It's so weird isn't it?'

'A little weird I suppose.'

'I used to fall asleep looking at it.' She reached up to touch it and the hem of her white blouse rose above her jeans. The fire crackled. I took a gulp of wine. I sensed a change had taken place while she was gone. It was a subtle change that neither of us was consciously aware of yet. But the air between us seemed now to be positively charged. Her written words came back to me: *When I'm lying in my bunk and looking at my painting of you, I think of how I want to touch you, and be touched by you.*

'So, how is your sister?' I repeated my question of earlier. Ruby sat down in the armchair farthest from me and tucked her bare feet beneath herself.

'She's fine. She gets emotional. More than me. But she's fine.' She took a sip of wine and started twirling her finger absent-mindedly through her hair.

I missed you. I was lonely when you left. I was afraid.

These were the thoughts that passed through my mind.

'What did you do together?'

'Nothing really. Just hung out at the house and talked. She asked me about you.'

'Me? What did she want to know?'

'Oh, you know, if you were normal. If you were good-looking.'

'What did you tell her?' Ruby let go of the strand of hair she'd been working on and it fell in a loose ringlet over her eye. She looked at me through it.

'Nothing to worry yourself about.' A loaded but not uncomfortable silence descended. On the first night she came it had been just me doing the spying. Now we took turns, it seemed, to look at one another over our wine glasses. I enjoyed the electricity of the moment and tried to ignore the seed of anxiety that had planted itself in my stomach.

'Something happened while you were gone,' I said.

'What?' Ruby sat more erect in the armchair and a hand went to her chest. She looked convincingly alarmed.

'Just some kids I think. Vandalised my shed with milk and eggs.'

'That's awful. Do you have any idea who would do that to you?'

'I don't know anyone round here. I've met Max Gray but I wouldn't say we know each other.'

'It *is* Halloween this month. Halloween makes some people act strange.'

I didn't mention the tyre track on the grass. Without the context of my recurring dream it didn't seem pertinent. And I couldn't mention the dreams without sounding crazy.

We drained a couple of bottles and when it was time for bed Ruby stumbled from wall to wall as though on a roiling ferry. There was a moment at the door to the box room – a lingering second in which she fixed my gaze and it seemed like she was waiting for me to say something – when it felt like all the cells in my body had suddenly squeezed together tightly. I couldn't move or speak. I could only look back into her eyes. She said goodnight, so softly, so quietly, almost a whisper.

The smell of wet paint roused me in the morning. I was badly hungover and the chemical aroma amplified the gnawing pain in my head. I emerged into the corridor to find Ruby, clad in an oversize T-shirt only, rolling white paint onto the wall.

'Morning,' she said gaily. 'Thought I'd get started.' She turned to face me. The T-shirt said BAD BITCH in black letters.

'Coffee?'

'Already had two. And I've fetched the eggs and milk. Fully intact today I'm happy to report.'

'Excellent.'

I went into the kitchen with my eyes half-closed.

'You look rough!' Ruby yelled. I hadn't the energy to yell back. I was leaning against the side waiting for the kettle to boil when she padded in barefoot. She pressed the back of her hand to my forehead.

'I'm not sick, I'm just hungover.'

'Here, sit down. Let me take care of you.'

'Why aren't *you* hungover?' I said, relenting and sitting at the table.

'I've never been hungover in my life.'

'I hate you.'

'Jade gets them. I don't. She hates me too.' She fixed me a strong coffee and then toast and eggs. She watched me eat it, tentatively at first, then with gusto. 'Feel better?' I nodded. 'Then you can help me paint.'

We were immediately back in the old routine, except now I spent more time with her in the cottage helping her whitewash the walls. Occasionally, she would go outside to smoke a cigarette. It was cold but I was happy to stand next to her. The days of this second week passed quickly. During the times that we were waiting for paint to dry we'd go to the living room and Ruby would sit in the rocking chair and read aloud to me. I liked the sound of her voice. She put on accents for the speech parts.

When she had to leave for her next Offender Manager meeting she announced that she would start painting more forest murals when she got back. 'Ivy will reclaim this house room by room,' she said. She left at six in the morning and was back at Lanes End by four that same afternoon. There wasn't time enough for me to fester like last time. Equally, there was no time for me to process my thoughts and feelings, which was maybe a blessing. Maybe living by my instincts would serve me better? But I did realise one thing in the ten or so hours that she was gone. I hadn't watched the video of Victoria all week.

There was no food in the pantry that we wanted to eat. Ruby suggested we go to a pub up the road. I had never once driven past a pub on the way to Lanes End.

'What pub?'

'It's called The Lighthouse.'

'Never heard of it.' I wondered where her local knowledge came from. 'They do food?'

'If you had internet we could check.'

'Well I'm starving so am willing to take a chance.'

'Shall we take my car?'

This was the first time I'd been driven by Ruby. When she'd turned the engine on, a CD played automatically. It was an American female voice talking. She ejected the disc immediately and dropped it into the door compartment next to her. But before she got to it I heard these words: *You are going to be OK. You are going ...*

'We don't need to hear that. How about some music instead?' She pressed a button and loud house music blasted from the speakers. Cringing at the noise she switched the unit off altogether. 'Or silence. How about just silence?'

We drove away from the cottage and turned left out of the gate. I had never driven this way before. There was never any reason to. Perhaps I'd been brought this way when I was a child? I had a vague memory of a sunny Sunday walk through Bowland Forest and a picnic eaten in the back of my father's van watching the rain. But the road east was a mystery to me now and I looked out upon this dark country like it was a foreign land. We drove past a stone house. This must've been the farmstead I saw when I came to after my accident. Ruby said it was Gray's place. There seemed no sign of life, even close up.

It didn't take long to reach The Lighthouse. It was a tiny stone building with four square little windows – two up, two down – which glowed warmly in the blue night. Ruby rolled carefully onto the gravel forecourt. A round wooden table sat unoccupied in the gloom, its sheathed parasol canting sadly to one side. We got out of the Mini and the sound of muffled male laughter reached our ears. There were a few cars parked. Vans too: a Peugeot Partner and a muddy white Transit. I did not see Gray's Land Rover. Ruby marched towards the door. As I followed her something on the other side of the Transit caught my eye: a pair of motorcycles parked on their kickstands next to each other.

'Come on then,' Ruby said, one hand on the door handle. I stood looking at the bikes. They were motocross bikes. Off-road bikes. 'My stomach's digesting itself.'

We opened the door and a choir of discordant voices hit us like a wave. We were standing in a hot little room filled exclusively with men. A few glanced at us. I saw one ginger-bearded man eyeballing Ruby as though she were the most exotic creature he'd ever laid eyes on. A man clutching three full pints of ale pushed through the crowd towards us, eyes down on the glasses, and we parted to let him by. Ruby said something but I didn't hear her. She leant in closer.

'It's rammed.'

'I'm not sure they'll do food here. It doesn't look like that kind of pub.'

'Let's just get a drink and then find somewhere a bit more out of the way to stand.'

'What do you want?' I said.

Waiting to be served by an old man in a dirty white shirt, I could see that the pub was separated into two rooms: the public bar where we were, and the saloon on the other side. The saloon looked far emptier. I could see just one man at the bar reading a tabloid and behind him a couple of men throwing darts. I ordered a pint of ale for me and a glass of dry white for Ruby. I asked the old man if they did food.

'Chips. Or these,' he said, pointing to the bags of pork scratchings and peanuts hanging behind him. I ordered some chips and found Ruby standing at a high round table in a corner near a fruit machine. She'd removed her jacket in the sweltering heat and slung it over her handbag, which dangled from a hook underneath the table. Her face was flushed and she fanned herself with a beer mat. I put the drinks down on the table. My left hand was wet with spilt ale. Ruby produced a tissue from her handbag.

'Come here,' she said. I looked at her as she worked the tissue into the crevices of my fingers. She was perspiring. When she was done I took the tissue from her and mopped her forehead. 'It's so hot.'

'I know,' I said. She took the tissue back from me and dropped it into her handbag.

'Cheers,' she said, raising her glass.

'Cheers,' I raised mine. A moment later a sour-faced teenager came over carrying a bowl.

'Chips?' she enquired.

'Yes thanks,' I said. The girl put the bowl on the table and disappeared back into the throng of men. 'What a lovely little place you've found here.'

'It's fine, let's just get hammered.'

'That's all right for you to say, you'll be fine in the morning, I'll be dead.'

And so we drank. Ruby switched to ale. She could certainly put it away. We drank more. And more. Eventually a high stool became available and Ruby pulled it over and sat up at the table like a queen surveying her motley court. We talked and laughed and I forgot about the motorcycles out front.

'Another?' she asked, jumping down from her throne. Was this the fifth pint or the sixth? There were fewer men now. Still, one or two watched her closely as she made her way to the bar. She was oblivious. I felt protective of her. I wanted to grab these men by their beards and pull their gaze in another direction. I wanted their sleazy eyes off her. At the bar the old man was serving someone already and I saw him gesture to Ruby that she was next. She leant her weight forward onto the bar. I saw then that she was talking to someone in the saloon bar on the other side. It was a very young-looking man, eighteen or nineteen. Who's to say he wasn't seventeen and being served anyway? He wore a black T-shirt with a yellow smiley face smoking a joint on it, and an army camo baseball cap tilted back on his head. A wispy moustache dressed his upper lip. He was smiling lewdly and saying something to Ruby. Impossible to make out over the din. She stretched up onto her tiptoes to try to hear him. I felt like I'd seen this boy before. He raised his pint to Ruby and she gave him a thumbs-up gesture. Then the old man came over and she pointed at the boy and the old man went away and brought back two dark shots. He gave one to the boy and one to Ruby. They each raised their glasses and then downed them. The boy then left some change on the bar and stood up, gesturing to someone out of sight. Then he grabbed his jacket and left. I turned away then. I was trembling with irrational possessive thoughts, with anger, with rampant jealousy. Ruby came over with two more pints. Why had he talked to Ruby? And why buy her a shot? Was it celebratory, a toast to my humiliation? The Lighthouse was entirely Ruby's idea. I'd never even heard of it. And now he was gone. To do more of her bidding? I wanted to grab Ruby by the shoulders, to shake her, to ask outright if she was Jade, if this was all a con, but another part of me desperately wanted to pull her flushed face towards me and kiss her. I did neither.

'Who was that ... at the bar?' I said, starting on the fresh pint.

'Who?'

'Just now. At the bar. You did ... shots.'

'Some lad. Wanted to buy me a drink so I let him.'

'I know him,' I said. I thought this might make her nervous, me knowing him. But she showed no hint of anxiety.

'Where from?'

'I don't know. I've seen him before. But I can't think ...'

'... Come on. Let's go,' she said, hopping down from the stool. Her chipper tone was infuriating. I sensed she knew I didn't want the conversation to end. She was being evasive. I wanted to have it out with her then and there. We were now almost alone in the pub. Only a group of three men playing dominoes at a low table remained. The old man had started putting stools upside down on tables. Ruby tottered as she stooped to unhook her handbag. Suddenly, her drunkenness irritated me. I rubbed my chin and felt the coarseness of burgeoning stubble. I craved the razor.

The air outside was cold. We stumbled towards the Mini. Ruby produced the key from her handbag and jangled it by her ear as though it were a tiny bell. I shook my head. But for Ruby's Mini, the car park was completely empty. The two motorcycles were gone too.

'You're smashed,' I said.

'*You're* smashed,' she said.

'We're walking,' I said.

The moon lit up the long straight road. We could see all the way to Gray's farm and beyond that the curve towards Lanes End. We walked in the middle of the road. Ruby's teeth chattered. I put my arm over her shoulder and held her to me. I felt her body shivering. She wrapped her arms around my waist under my jacket. Her head was pressed to my chest. A smell like almonds. We stumbled along silently like a three-legged creature swaying left and right. Ditches and thorny hedges lined the road. Behind them fields and fields separated us from everything; the great bay to our right, the hills to our left. The sea was invisible but making itself heard, a whisper on the air. When we reached Gray's farm there were no lights on but bass-heavy music was coming from somewhere.

Eventually, we came to Lanes End. Ruby ripped the anti-fracking sign from the ground and held it aloft triumphantly.

'No fracking here! Leave our land alone!' she cried. I watched her, laughing despite my earlier anger. She began spinning around with the sign in her hand in a crazy waltz. She let go and flung the sign away like an Olympic hammer and fell into me with such force that we ended up in a heap on the ground. 'Are you alright?' she said. I couldn't speak, the wind had gone from my lungs, but I gave her a thumbs-up. She shuffled nearer to me and began stroking my forehead. 'I'm so sorry.' We were so close, her face was only a couple of inches from mine. Her fingers kneaded my forehead with a featherlight touch. Slowly, tenderly. And we paused like that. But then I saw the look in her eyes change, swiftly, almost imperceptibly, and as though a spell had been broken my breath suddenly returned. I sat upright and

Ruby rubbed my back until I could breathe normally. 'Let's get inside,' she said, rising clumsily to her feet, and offered me her hand.

We walked side by side now, not pressed together as we had been on the road. The woods clicked and whistled. The lane was crunchy and hard. Ruby was a step ahead of me, tramping unsteadily, her red leather jacket grey in the gloom. Something had passed between us back there, on the ground, and though I wanted to speak, to grab this thing before it escaped completely, reserve held me back. Soon we reached the end of the lane and the cottage sat before us.

'Is the kitchen light on?' Ruby said, stopping in her tracks. I stopped too.

'I must have left it on,' I said. Ruby backed slowly into me.

'No, that's not right.' She was whispering now.

'I *must* have done. Or else you did.'

'No, I remember switching it off before we left.'

'Are you sure?'

'Yes. I specifically remember switching it off.'

'Maybe Alfred ...'

'... I don't find this funny, Dan.'

'OK, OK. There must be an explanation,' I said and began walking towards the side door. I slid the key in the door and slowly turned the handle. Ruby clung to my coat. I did not switch on the corridor light, I went straight to the sitting room because from there you could look straight through to the kitchen. As I turned the door handle I could see Ruby had a steak knife in her hand. The same one I had found, the one I had put in the drawer? I pushed open the door and crept through the sitting room, Ruby just behind, clutching her weapon. The grandfather clock tick-tocked in the corner. Sure enough the kitchen light was on. But that wasn't the thing that shocked me most.

'Oh god,' Ruby said, not whispering any more. The back door was wide open. I pulled it shut and locked it. An expression of terror drew itself across Ruby's face, her mouth becoming an oval.

'What, Ruby? What is it?' I went to her and placed the palm of my hand on her cheek. Her wild wide eyes frightened me.

'It's him! He must have heard I'm out.'

'You mean ...?'

'He must've tracked me down. Oh, god!' She lowered herself into a chair beside the clock.

'That's not possible.'

'Why not? *I* found you.'

'Then we should call the police,' I said, rummaging in my inside jacket pocket for the Nokia. Ruby leapt to her feet.

'No, don't!' she cried, and tried to grab the phone from me. 'Please don't ... don't do that.'

'Why not? If you think you're being stalked by your ex then we should report it.'

'We just *can't* call the police about this.'

'Ruby, this is crazy.'

'Dan,' she took my face in both of her hands and looked into my eyes. My instinct was to put her on the spot and force her to explain. 'Please, Dan, just trust me.' It made no sense not to call the police if she had nothing to hide. I suspected she had orchestrated this 'incident' herself, intentionally leaving the light on, the back door open. But why? And why bring Lee up? I was bewildered. My thoughts led nowhere, resolved to nothing. I felt like a rat in a maze, entangled in a scheme too complicated for me to understand. The only thing I felt certain of was that this was yet another reason not to trust her.

'Tomorrow I'll change the locks,' I announced, 'if it makes you feel safe.' She burrowed into me like a tiny animal.

I was stirred in the night by the sound of my bedroom door creaking open. I froze, half-hoping that it was a dream, and squeezed my eyes shut. Then, soft padding footsteps made their way over to my bed. Then, a wave of cold air on my bare legs as the sheet was lifted. Then, a pair of arms, folded like wings, tucked themselves softly into my back. Then, one of the arms opened and draped over my body. She wriggled closer to me until her body was pressed flat against mine. I could feel her breath on my neck. I could feel her heart beating. I lay still, trying to preserve this sensation. Just before I fell asleep in a bubble of warmth I had a thought: was this simply to make sure I didn't call the police behind her back? If it was, in that moment I didn't care.

**

Robbie called today. But it was not a normal visit. He came in, switched the telly on, turned the volume up, but didn't look at it. He was wincing, pressing a hand to his stomach. I asked if he was feeling all right. He ignored me. His eye is looking much better these days. It's still swollen but at least it's stopped seeping. He increased the volume even further. Is his hearing going now too? I thought. Every so often he would clutch at his stomach and emit a low growl. Then, when whatever it was had passed, he'd continue on. This happened a number of times. I could not ignore it.

'Jesus Robbie you're sick,' I said.

'Oh god.' He was bent double. 'It'll pass,' he said holding his arm out and keeping very still.

'Do you want some water?' I said, half-rising from the desk. He shook his head and very slowly started to unfold himself. He settled gingerly back on the bed and continued with his story. He didn't get very far before he was seized by another attack.

'Fuck!' Robbie grabbed at his stomach with his fingers like he was trying to pull something out.

'Shit Robbie, you really need to see a doctor,' I said.

'Honestly, Danny … it's nothing,' he said.

'Robbie, that's not nothing, you need a doctor.'

I stood up and made for the door but somehow Robbie found the energy to leap across the room to block me. He shouted in my face: 'NO!' one hand in my chest the other dug deep into his stomach, 'Sit back down and don't even fucking think about it.' His voice was demented. He stood in the doorway like a troll, bent, his good eye squinting against the pain. 'I don't need a doctor.'

I was trembling. I've never seen that side of him before. He just snapped. Lost it. I lowered myself into my chair with my hands raised in surrender. He looked at me out of his bad eye, then up at the telly, then back down at me, and then he turned and left.

***

As promised I changed the locks and installed anti-theft devices on the windows. Ruby had me go outside to simulate someone trying to jimmy them. Though she still looked fraught she seemed satisfied. If this was a ruse it was an elaborate one. I kept the thought to myself that these locks would make no difference against a brick.

We did not speak of the night before. Not because

lying together was forbidden. We did not speak of it simply because there was no need to. It had felt right to do it. It felt safe. In the morning Ruby had awoken with a long decadent yawn. I turned to face her. Her plum red hair was splayed over her face and pillow in every direction like a trampled bouquet. She let me rearrange it while she lay there with her eyes closed.

Wasting no time, Ruby got on with her project, the pretext which had kept her here. I stood and watched her use my pencil – a carpenter's most important tool, my father used to say – to transfer the flora and fauna in her mind onto the whitewashed walls, which she then gave colour and depth to with the brush. She painted adroitly. Under her careful supervision I added small details; the dots on a beetle's wing, the stamen of a flower. She was a good instructor and inspired in me a desire to please her. This must have been how she was with her patients, with Lee. It was in moments like this that I grew more convinced of her story. I wanted it all to be true. Even, yes, the atrocities. Because if they were real, then *this* was real. Don't misunderstand, the sceptic within me was still there, still whispering its incessant suspicions. I had simply stuffed a sock in its mouth.

The rainforest extended out from the nursery, leaf by leaf, vine by vine along the corridor, as though it was a living expanding thing. We stood back to admire our work.

'See, it's growing,' she said.

The next day a chain of wet days began that would last the whole week. There was something of the quality of school summer holidays to those days. Outwardly we cursed the rain's siege but secretly we savoured the enforced closeness. Cooped up indoors together in our socks with the sound of the rain on the shale and the roof, I could feel the bond between us growing stronger. We were fuzzy from the lack of fresh air but fearful of one day having to venture outside again in case this spell should be broken. We did not wear shoes the entire week, except for the daily dash for the eggs and milk. Ruby squealed as she ran back to the cottage, cutting across the clearing as I waited for her inside the door with a towel.

The ivy grew quickly in the rain. We slept in my bed together every night and wore the same paint-spattered clothes every day. At night we talked about places Ruby wanted to travel to. Her eyes lit up with talk of Morocco and Tibet and Peru. I was jealous of these places, jealous of the extinct tribes and dead heroes which captured her imagination and lured her thoughts away. I wanted us to stay here like this forever. Some nights she wrapped her arms over my body and other nights I wrapped mine over hers and she took my hand and held it to her stomach.

'Have you seen Alfred lately?' Ruby said one afternoon, her brush poised in the air before the pencil outline of an exotic bird. I realised I hadn't seen or heard Alfred since the break-in. Recently, I had taken to putting larger piles of feed in his cage, enough to sustain him for longer periods, and I hadn't been into the nursery to inspect it in days. There had been interludes of absence like this since I had let him free, but when Ruby said those words I suddenly sensed something wrong. His food was still piled high in a mound, undisturbed. We searched every room calling his name over and over but there was no sign of him. I even shone my torch up the chimney. We might've unwittingly roasted him. He wasn't there. Since I changed the locks we hadn't left any windows or doors open at any point, so he couldn't have just flown away.

Tomorrow Ruby was returning to Stoke for another meeting and when we went to bed there was a new and unfamiliar quality to the atmosphere. Alfred's disappearance was a pinprick to the bubble in which we'd been living and we regarded each other over the bed warily, suddenly hyperaware of each another. That night for the first time we lay facing each other. She burrowed into the nook of my neck. I felt her mouth move over my skin. Was this a kiss? Her lips moved so gently it was impossible to tell.

I woke in the night needing the toilet. Ruby wasn't

in bed. In the corridor I saw her shoes were gone. The wax jacket had been removed from its hook. I opened the door. There was soft rain and a full moon. The Mini was parked in its usual place. I got back into bed and tried to stay awake for her return but I was too tired and soon fell asleep. I stirred when she came back and wriggled near to me. She felt cold and her hair smelt like pine.

The following morning Ruby found Alfred's body by the gate. She brought it back with the milk and eggs, placed it on the kitchen table. His spine was broken. He'd been practically folded in half. The image of Lee's broken body flashed into my head. She said she found him propped up against the bottle of milk. I sat down and she put her hands on my shoulders.

'I'm so sorry,' she said. I stayed quiet for a long time listening to my thoughts. I thought through the sequence of events on the night of the pub. I thought of the steak knife she had produced so suddenly when we had come back from the pub. Where was it now? 'I think it was Lee,' she said suddenly, as though sensing the path my mind was on and trying to divert it. She lowered herself delicately into the chair next to me. 'It's him. He's found me.' She began to cry. As the tears fell she fixed her gaze on me, making a display of her emotion. 'Dan, I'm scared.' She squeezed my hands. 'I'm scared,' she repeated.

'Does he ride a motorbike?'

'What?' she asked, screwing up her pinkened face in vexation.

'Does Lee ride a motorbike?'

'He didn't when we were together. Why?'

'Then I don't think it's him.' I explained then about the motorcycle engines I'd been hearing and the skid mark on the grass and the two motorcycles on their kickstands outside The Lighthouse. 'Alfred's killer was probably in the pub when we were. They'll have nabbed him while we were out. But who would want to terrorise me like this? I don't know anyone well enough to make an enemy out of them.'

'Strange,' Ruby said. She was calmer now, sheepish even. She looked down at her hands. 'Maybe people around here just don't like newcomers?'

I thought of the Brexit sign and considered that she might have a point. But I was a Wild' un, born in the area, and Gray had been giving me surplus from his farm this whole time.

I looked at Alfred's broken body on the table, his luminous green plumage flecked with mud. 'We should bury him.'

I wrapped him in a gingham tea towel and put him in a jar. I made a hole in the sand and buried him under a pile of his favourite pebbles.

Back inside the cottage Ruby said she had to set off

or else risk missing her next appointment, which was later that day. Sullenly, I said it was OK. I sat at the kitchen table and listened to her potter about packing her things. And then she came and kissed my cheek, like a wife leaving for work, and said she'd be back that evening. I heard the side door close and I was alone. With Alfred gone there was nothing of my old life left.

This was the twenty-second of October.

When she came back that evening the rain had stopped. The first time in a week.

In the night she disappeared. I found her sitting outside smoking a cigarette. She was wearing the waxed jacket. The night sky was clear, a dome of indigo speckled with October stars. You could see the curve of space.

'Some nights I could see the stars from my cell,' she said, 'if it was clear like tonight and I put my head at the foot of my bunk. It's hard to believe these are the same ones.' Beside her lay her Nokia and the little dark book. Who had she been calling so late? She put out her cigarette and stood up crookedly. She stooped to pick up her mobile and notebook. She walked towards me and placed an icy hand on my arm. 'That one's the North Star,' she said, pointing to a throbbing silvery dot in the sky. 'If you can see that, you're not lost.'

That night I dreamt I was inside Ruby's mural, working through the thick undergrowth with a box of razor blades tucked under my arm. I hacked and slashed, using a fresh blade for every vine – I had an unlimited supply. The cut vines bled onto the rainforest floor. I was trying to get somewhere. I had a goal. I became aware that my face was lacerated each time I cut a vine. My cheeks and chin stung and I had dripped a trail of blood behind me.

The next morning Ruby issued the decree that we ought to go 'all out' for Halloween. Then she said those things about honouring the dead and saints and martyrs that I mentioned earlier. And so, for a week leading up to her next appointment on the twenty-ninth, we began dressing up the house. Ruby had a vision for Lanes End, which she executed – despite the tackiness of the season – with artistic flair. She had me cut orange and black pieces of craft paper into strips and glue them together in loops so they formed long chains, metres and metres of them, which we hung from the ceiling. She had me paint various slogans on offcuts of sheet timber like: KEEP OUT! ENTER AT YOUR OWN RISK! TURN BACK NOW! which we mounted on stakes by the gate.

'Let's spook them away, whoever is fucking with us,' she said, delivering the final mallet blow. I made crosses out of the wooden slats of the disassembled cot and turned the clearing into a 'cemetery'. One of the slats had DANIEL carved into it and I gave this 'grave' prominence. We painted other names on the crosses too: Alfred, Ivy, her father's name and mine. She created lanterns from orange crepe paper. She cut spiders out of black card that looked like they were crawling up the walls. She erected a sheet ghost in the corridor. She made 'spooky' boiled sweets. When it was all done she wasn't satisfied. 'It's tame,' she said. So I brought out from the workshop a number of bottles – bleach, paint thinner, lacquer – and we re-labelled them: ACID, DANGER, CORROSIVE SUBSTANCE, DO NOT DRINK, and so on, and displayed them on the sides in the kitchen and in the sitting room. She had me fetch tools: pliers, chisel hammers, hacksaws and so on, and lay them out on a tea tray like a surgeon's implements, which was set out on the coffee table. Using one of the hammers herself, she drove nails into the beams in the corridor and hung nooses, made out of an old hosepipe, from them. 'There,' she said, 'much better.'

A few hours later, whilst cutting out what felt like my millionth paper bat by the fire, I heard Ruby emit a sort of animal wail in the corridor. I ran to her.

'What is it?' She was clutching a piece of paper. She would not look up at me or respond in any way. Her hand was clasped to her mouth. I touched her shoulder. 'What's wrong?'

'It's him. I told you.'

'What are you talking about?'

'Look.' She gave me the paper and turned away from it as though it were toxic, as though she couldn't bear to see it. I unfolded the note.

I never forgot you did you forget me?? It must mean something that I never forgot you even after what you did to me! Who is this other [illegible]? I don't trust him. It was only a few [illegible] we [illegible] each other I only ever tried to protect you from the world I have forgiven you three and [illegible] years is ages gives me time to think and I forgive you and I will always love you and am HERE FOR YOU NOW I want you to know this.
Lee

It was water-damaged and some of the words were smudged and could not be read. But I got the gist. Lee was back. Lee had tracked her down. Lee was '*HERE ... NOW*'. I admit, I was alarmed. But at the same time I didn't really believe in it. The picture Ruby had painted of Lee was not of a stunted delinquent with an infantile scrawl. The letter seemed too melodramatic to be genuine, too obviously crazed, just as her initial Halloween decorations were too gaudy, too schlocky to scare anyone. She was pressing both palms to the wall now and hanging her head between her arms and breathing deeply in through her nose and out of her mouth. If she had forged the letter, what action had it been designed to provoke? What feelings? Pity? Love?

I wanted so much to screw the note into a ball, to hurl it at her, eject her from my house, from my life. Instinct told me to do this. But I could not. Something always seemed to hold me back when it came to Ruby. Something like a fog descended. I wanted to walk one way, but when the fog cleared, I'd end up having walked miles in the opposite direction.

'Where did this come from?'

'It was in the letter box,' she said between breaths.

'Where's the envelope?'

'What?'

'The envelope. It'll have a postmark on it. Maybe we can trace where it came from.'

'There was no envelope.'

'It was just there? This little note? In the letterbox?'

'I told you, Dan. I told you, but you wouldn't believe me. He's really found me. He's really here. Out there somewhere.'

I watched her, chest heaving, attempting to control her breaths, and I felt the heat of anger cooled by a sudden wave of sadness. For I was beginning to recognise as truth what I had long suspected. That Ruby was not just a master manipulator – she was mad. That she was desperate for someone, some man, to take her and make her the Centre of His Universe. Her troubled relationship with her father was perhaps the only thread of truth in this whole tapestry. I was also sure that she had been in prison. But not of the reason why. And not of the duration. Probably everything else she had ever told me was a lie. Stoke. Art Psychotherapy. Lee. Jade. Yes, it was beginning to make sense now.

There *was* no Jade.

Jade. The projection of the person Ruby wished to be, of the person she thought her *father* wished her to be. The two Facebook accounts suddenly made sense. They were both Ruby! Ruby playing the role she had envisaged and created for herself, taking on the persona she inside felt she deserved but wasn't capable of sustaining. Pretending to be an art psychotherapist was an integral part of it, a way for her to enjoy a form of control and influence over people as she could never hope to as her true self. Who else had she fooled?

Jade. The other precious stone, glowing green with serenity and goodness, the antithesis to the red ruby of fire, blood and death. The fantasy of a rejected child. An obvious choice.

I felt then the familiar weight of bereavement press against my chest. I had lost Ruby. She was gone, a ghost, a projection of my own. She was never really here. I looked at the note again, at the obviously faked handwriting. It was all fake. And was I any better than her, for having played along when in the back of my mind

I sensed something wasn't right? It was an impossible, screwed-up mess.

How I needed Victoria now. Wanted, craved her.

I could scarcely believe how stupid I had been, how self-destructive. I needed to overcome this, my weakness for her, and find a way to extricate myself from this car crash. But then I looked at her and I heard myself saying:

'I'm here. Nothing is going to happen. You're safe with me. I'll report it, OK? Nothing will happen.'

After a storm of tears, she assumed a vacant calm. I went into the bedroom to 'call the police' and she went into the kitchen to 'call Jade'. We didn't speak again about the note.

In the days that followed I noticed a rabbitlike twitchiness about her whenever she caught me watching her watching the treeline or hear a sound outdoors, which made me wonder if she knew I knew, and whether her act had moved into a new and more delusional phase.

I made a show of keeping the doors and windows locked and this seemed to pacify her.

The night of the twenty-eighth I found her in the kitchen carving a face into a pumpkin. She'd been doing this all week. There was a pyramid of them in the pantry: a gallery of faces in various poses of anguish. The knife was sharp and I winced as she tried to force it through the pumpkin's tough exterior.

'Why do we need so many pumpkins?' I asked.

'These aren't pumpkins, they're jack-o'-lanterns.' The blade slipped. She stumbled forward slightly. 'Their light protects us from the undead, from vampires. The devil.'

'OK.'

'You don't believe in it?'

'In what? Vampires?'

'Evil.' She began stabbing the pumpkin, chipping at a hole she'd somehow managed to make without slicing off her finger.

'I believe there are evil people.'

'But where does evil come from? The Devil, of course.'

'That'd be a convenient explanation for some.'

'Where else could it come from? Who wakes up one morning and suddenly decides to be evil?'

'I think people become evil over time, maybe because of things that happen to them.'

'I think that's an even more convenient explanation. Would you forgive Frank for what he did to your mother if you found out he had a rough childhood? I would never forgive Lee no matter what he went through before.' The mention of Frank made me shudder. I stroked my chin and was relieved to feel it smooth. She plunged the knife forcefully into the widening hole, then looked at me with a smug smile on her face, a smile that said:

you know I'm right. And I did. And if I was to die or be maimed by her hand perhaps I deserved it, perhaps the Devil had got into me.

'I'm sorry,' I said. Her stabbing ceased. She held the knife deep inside the pumpkin's core and was twisting it.

'What for?'

I paused. 'For everything.'

'I'm sorry too,' she said.

The next morning, the twenty-ninth, Ruby left again to meet her 'Offender Manager'. She'd sold the lie so now she had to keep it going, I supposed. But if I was going to catch her out, I had to bide my time. I waved her off with a smile.

I spent the rest of the day finishing off the trunks. The only thing left to do was secure the safety hinges. As I locked the workshop door I realised I hadn't fired the laptop up in weeks. It hadn't even occurred to me to. It lay cold and unused in the drawer.

Ruby returned that night with costumes.

On the thirtieth I woke up and through bleary eyes watched Ruby stir and felt a strong and fervid affection churn in my belly. She held the palm of her hand to my cheek. She had such talent for make-believe. I was able in such moments of semi-wakefulness, of almost-dreaming, to suspend my disbelief. To pull the delusion nearer, to wrap it around my face like a blanket, to obscure everything beyond it. I close my eyes and 'Ruby' is here and the world and its truth are not.

It was the day before Halloween. This the thing that drove all of our mad endeavours over the course of that sweet and unreal day. She baked cinnamon-spiced pumpkin cupcakes with black icing that made your teeth 'rot', wrapped the cooled boiled sweets in plastic wrappers, and around midday made a start on the punch. By four o'clock we were drunk. The hours of that tipsy afternoon in the warm kitchen disappeared in a blink, as though time itself experienced a sugar rush. I can still picture Ruby's teeth, blackened from the cupcakes, smiling. At dusk she said she was going for a little wander, to clear her head. An hour or so passed. She had been gone longer than usual. Anxiety brought sobriety. I began to pace, to fidget, to tidy. At around six, stood at the kitchen sink washing dishes, I sensed something out in the pines. I turned the light off (with it on I could see only my reflection) and stared into the dark trees but I could see nothing. I opened the back door and walked over the strip of shale to the edge of the pines. I called Ruby's name. No reply. I turned to look back at the cottage, at the open door to the kitchen. Something felt wrong. I walked back inside, locked the door behind me and resumed the dishes. At that moment Ruby emerged from the woods. She was wearing the waxed jacket. There was something in her right hand. Seeing me in the kitchen window she froze. I expected her to smile or wave but she did not. She just stood there looking at me. Then I saw that it was a knife she held. A short blade, a steak knife. After a couple more seconds she walked with purpose away from the pines. I followed the crunching of her steps until they disappeared. And then I heard the side door opening and her footsteps continue through the cottage towards me in the kitchen. I turned to face the door, noting the location of the rolling pin which I had just cleaned, and tried to smile as she came bounding towards me.

'Look what I found,' she said, producing a cluster of small green apples from the pockets of the wax jacket. 'Did you know you have apple trees?' I said nothing. I just watched her put the apples on a chopping board and begin to cut them, using a kitchen knife from the drying rack behind me. She ate a segment and smiled blissfully. 'They're good. Here.' She placed a piece of apple in my mouth. 'See?' The apple could have been the best I'd ever tasted, but all I could think about was where she'd put the steak knife.

After a dinner of pumpkin pie we sat on cushions by the fire and Ruby read aloud from *Wuthering Heights*, which she'd taken up again and which she was nearing the end of.

I pictured Heathcliff wandering forlornly through

the empty rooms of the house he had strived his whole life to acquire through crazy love and revenge, and which welcomed him now emptily, coldly; a lavish and austere tomb. I looked up at Ruby's face, which was only inches from mine. Noticing my gaze she stopped reading and lowered the book. Impulsively, I placed my hands on either side of her head and drew her to me. She looked shocked at my sudden decisive gesture but did not resist me. I kissed her lips then and we rose to our feet, like two vines colliding and rising up from the ground, twined together. And as we moved from the living room into the coolness of the bedroom, I pictured leaves of ivy emerging all over our bodies. As we lay down in the bed I pictured the ivy spreading from us onto the bed, across the floor, through the gaps in the door, the corridors and into every room, covering every wall inside and out until the whole cottage was swallowed entirely by ivy and we were its beating heart.

I slept easily. But in the night I was disturbed by the sound of footsteps outside. I staggered naked to the window. I stood for about a minute, scanning the treeline for movement. I was about to give up and get back into bed when a figure emerged from behind the shed. A gangly man wearing a motorcycle helmet. He walked to the edge of the clearing, as though deliberately showing himself to me, and just stood there. A second man – also wearing a motorcycle helmet – came out from the trees lining the driveway. Was this a message, a threat? Or a final intake of breath before the assault? After a few moments they went, not turning and walking away but moving slowly backwards in the manner of spirits, swallowed by the black trees.

In the morning there was no power. The fuse box had been tampered with. Wires had been cut. I didn't tell Ruby, I just said a fuse had blown. She didn't care. She thought it was exciting. She went around lighting candles and jack-o'-lanterns, which she placed outside so they 'protected' the cottage. The gas was still working and we had scrambled eggs and coffee for breakfast by candlelight. After breakfast I showered in cold water and attempted to dress but was intercepted by Ruby brandishing my vampire costume on its hanger. As I put it on, something about it made me feel uneasy, something beyond mere embarrassment. I couldn't put my finger on it.

'I'm going to get the milk,' I said, emerging from the bedroom.

'Make sure you avoid direct sunlight.' She found my discomfort delicious.

My transition into the monstrous under way, I trudged up the lane through the woods to the gate. I had the sense that things were coming to a head, that today something was going to happen. Her seduction of me.

Our sleeping together. The motorcyclists in the night. I got to the gate and found the milk but no eggs. I stood for a moment at the roadside, my cape flapping in the wind. The road was lined with dead leaves. The bottle was freezing my fingers. As I turned to go back I noticed the flag on the mailbox was up. I opened the flap and saw a single folded sheet. It was unaddressed. I recognised the handwriting immediately. Here is what I read:

Dan

Everything's a mess. I need to see you. I need to talk to you. You have every right to hate me, but I'll go crazy if I don't speak to you. There's so much I need to say to you. Sorry for starters.

Will you see me? Will you speak to me if I come? I didn't think I had a right simply to waltz up and knock on your front door; I thought you at least deserved the courtesy of a note first. I'll come tomorrow, at noon. If there's any feeling left inside your heart for me at all I hope you can keep it alive until then.

Love

Vic

In a flash everything was made clear.

It was Victoria I loved, of course it was. But I was still trussed up here with Ruby, hanging from a hook of my own making.

If she saw Ruby it would be the end.

Tomorrow, the note said, meaning today. *Noon*.

A deadline.

It had to end now.

***

Robbie was waiting for me when I got back from the workshop yesterday. He stood at my door wringing an invisible cap in his hands and began immediately to plead for forgiveness. I told him to forget about it, it was nothing. He sat on the bed and switched on the telly. We caught the tail end of *Loose Women*, in which the panel was enjoying a typically discursive chat ranging from Colombia's rejection of a peace deal with FARC to their dismay over the break-up of a popular pairing from *Celebrity Love Island*. Robbie began to talk obliquely about love and regret. I recorded his babblings in my notepad because no one else ever will. I have become in a sense his biographer.

After he'd tired himself out talking about the past he continued watching telly. In a lull there was a sound like a mobile phone vibrating. We looked at each other. He knew I'd heard it. It happened again. Robbie plunged his hand into his pocket. He was rummaging for something. He looked stricken then, the vibrating continuing and he unable to stop it. I couldn't hide my shock. He jumped up from the bed, his pocket emitting the telltale sound, pulled the tiny impossible thing out, pressed a button to silence it and stuffed it back inside his pocket. He looked at me, sweat gathering like an avalanche over his protruding brow, turning some decision over in his mind, and ran out.

Last night, unable to sleep, I was looking out across the grass towards the treeline. I was thinking about Robbie and what he could be mixed up in and whether in seeing the mobile phone I had embroiled myself in it like a fly in a pot of jam. I thought about the note under my door and his disappearance and grisly resurrection, and as I groped blindly inside this box of sundry clues I felt the outlines of a theory beginning to emerge. But before I could gather it in my hands a commotion broke out outside. A black figure (I *had* seen it before!) darted right to left, away from the chain-link fence separating the grass from the walking path. Then another figure emerged from a hiding place in the trees, wielding a torch. This second figure was shouting 'STOP!' at the black figure, who covered the ground impossibly quickly. The man with the torch could not keep up and it seemed the fleer would escape but then a third man emerged from the left and between the two of them they pincered him and wrestled him to the ground. The two men, police I gather, marched their quarry across the grass out of sight and then another couple of officers came walking ponderously out onto the grass pointing torches at the ground, crackly robotic voices issuing from their radios.

***

I had no time to reproach myself for having slept with Ruby, for making her removal a thousand times more difficult. The clock was ticking. *Noon.* With Vic's note in my hand I hurried back to the cottage. I had no plan. It was all I could do to hold the panic at bay, to prevent it from controlling me totally.

Maybe I could call Victoria, put her off coming, or at least slow her down? I still had her number saved but I'd left the Nokia in the bedroom. I would have to make the call in secret. Otherwise there would be questions: who are you calling, why? And if I invented some reason – I was calling my client, or the timber merchant, or the electricity board – the phone call with Vic would take much longer than any such call feasibly would; plus there was no guarantee I would be successful and Victoria might come anyway. But I had to try. I had no better ideas.

I crunched over the shale and slipped in through the side door. I listened. Ruby was clattering around in the kitchen, completely preoccupied. A reprieve. I sidled along the corridor towards the bedroom door, wincing at the rustle of the cheap polyester cape behind me. In the bedroom I set the bottle of milk down, closed the door as softly as I could and tiptoed to the bay window with the Nokia, where the signal was strongest. I dialled 'Vic Mob'. It rang and rang. *Come on!* I looked at the screen: CALLING: Vic Mob. No answer. Not even an answering machine. It had been months since we'd spoken, maybe she had a new number. There was one other option: Vic Work. I hit CALL. It was picked up immediately.

'Wilder Road Dental Practice,' said the female voice.

'Hello,' I whispered, 'is Vic working today?'

'Sorry what was that?'

'Is Vic working?'

'Sorry who?'

'Victoria,' I hissed, cupping my mouth.

'Sorry one sec,' she said and put me on hold. The old familiar jingle. How many times had I waited for her – not quite like this – to come to the work phone in the past? I began to drift off into memory, into a montage of a previous life, small, meaningless conversations; do we need milk, when are you going to your mum's, where's …

'Sorry sir, no one called Victoria works here.'

'What? What are you talking about?'

'Sorry one sec.'

'Who is this?' said another female voice. Older. Familiar.

'It's Dan.'

'Dan! Hi, it's Miriam. How are you? How's Vic doing?'

'That's why I'm calling.'

'We haven't heard from her since she was signed off. We're worried about her. Sorry about Jen, she's temping while Vic is away. She doesn't know.'

'Signed off?'

'Well, yes. Dan, is something wrong?'

'How long?'

'Dan are you joking? She's been signed-off on long-term sick since the beginning of October.'

I froze. I couldn't compute what Miriam was saying. I was unable to formulate words. I hung up.

My plan had failed. Vic would be here soon and I was left now with only one option.

I had to hide Ruby.

I had to find a way to take Ruby out of the equation and manage Victoria so their paths didn't cross. Then, when Victoria left (she'd eventually have to leave for something) I would just have to bite the bullet and break it off with Ruby (I had accepted now there was no way to mitigate the risk of Ruby's reaction being explosive). But how to keep her out of sight? Since 'Lee's note' she virtually never ventured outside alone, so perhaps I could take Vic down to the rock pools? But this brought risk. Vic might be suspicious: Why can't we go to the cottage? Do you have company? It was very cold, and she might flat out refuse. And while it was unlikely Ruby would come looking for me, it wasn't impossible. Perhaps I could meet Vic at the gate and pretend that I wasn't 'ready' to have her come into the house yet, that I just wanted to talk for now, that the wound inflicted by her affair was still so raw that we'd have to take things slowly to begin with and perhaps we could meet somewhere neutral tomorrow and talk more, et cetera? But this would take time and Ruby might wonder where I was and could more easily find us there than at the rock pools.

The clock was ticking. Sixty minutes until noon. I was standing now with one palm pressed to the door. I had to do something. I chucked the Nokia on the bed, picked up the milk and reached for the doorknob. I was about to go out on stage still with no real plan, but at least with a concept. Hide her. At all costs get her out of sight.

I opened the door and went through to the kitchen. Ruby was now in full costume. Replete in tattered and torn white wedding dress and veil. A demon bride. Blood-spattered and grimed. Smokey make-up over one eye denoting a fierce conjugal beating. I knew as soon as I looked at her that I did not love her. Not truly. It was love with no future. Whereas my love for Victoria seemed in that moment to be brought back to life by the sight of Ruby as a corpse.

Love is sacred, Lucy. When you believe you have it you do everything you can to preserve it. Sometimes this means doing things that other people don't understand, can't understand. So you see, the thing I did next I did out of love.

'You look ridiculous,' Ruby said, as I walked past her to put the milk in the fridge.

'Is it too early to have a drink?'

'I usually wait until midday. But today I'll make an exception.'

'Good. A toast then.' I grabbed a half-finished bottle of wine from the pantry and poured two glasses. 'To our dead, our martyrs and our saints,' I said. We touched glasses and drank. I was in a state of such nervous excitement that I spilt a few drops on the floor and on my hand. I was standing where the dead mouse had been; its stain was still faintly visible in the candlelight.

Was that a sound outside? The crunching of shale? I thought. It can't be, her note said noon, it was only five past eleven. The sound was nothing. But urgency pressed against my skin now, painfully, like a blunt needle.

'Are you all right?' Ruby asked.

'Me? Oh yes, I'm fine. Wine is good in the morning isn't it?'

'You don't seem fine.'

'I'm just a little overexcited I think. There's

something I want to show you.' What was I saying? 'Come with me.' The words and actions came to me unbidden by any conscious thought. *When we ignore our instincts, that's when we get into trouble*, Ruby had said to me. And at this moment, it really seemed like I was being driven by some deep and elemental instinct.

'Where are we going?' Ruby asked. I didn't know myself. I led her by the hand through the sitting room into the corridor and towards the side door.

'Just wait and see.' When I opened the door I stopped. The day was so still. I looked around. A line of glowing jack-o'-lanterns led my eye from the side door across the shale to the workshop. I picked the keys up from the hook by the door and made a beeline for it.

'Oh, am I finally going to get a peek inside your man cave?' We marched arm in arm across the shale, Dracula and his reanimated bride, Ruby's tatty skirts sweeping shabbily over the ground. At the door I removed my top hat. 'This is all very mysterious, Dan.' I unlocked the padlock and kept it – and the key, still inside it – in my hand. I opened the door, slowly, theatrically, fixing Ruby's gaze. She feigned a frightened shiver.

'You may enter,' I said. As she did so I turned on the light. Ruby gasped. I went inside after her, leaving the door open behind me.

'Look at all this stuff.' She went around the work-shop touching things, bits of wood, bits of metal, my chisels, my hatchet. I had begun backing slowly towards the door. Ruby was digging her hands into the little pots of nails and screws mounted on the wall, pulling the roll of sandpaper from its spool like loo paper, kicking sawdust around like autumn leaves. How easy it would be just to leave her there, to close the door and quickly click the padlock into place. She'd take it as a Hallow-een trick. She'd play along, expecting more tricks. Then how easy it would be to say: *oops the rotten old key's broken off in the padlock*, and: *just wait here*, buying the time I needed to covertly dispatch Victoria. Just then Ruby noticed the trunks lined up along the front wall. She inspected them. I watched her from the door.

'Is this what you've been working on this whole time?' she asked, placing her palm on the lid of the trunk closest to her as though feeling for a heartbeat. She opened the lid and stooped to fill her nose with the smell of cut wood and varnish. 'They're bigger than they look inside.' She put one bare foot and then the other into the trunk. Then she crouched down. 'I fit easily,' she announced, her voice eerily amplified. She went to stand up again but lost her balance and fell back down. The lid closed on top of her with a bang. She began bashing frantically against it but the hasp had come down over the locking eye and the lid wouldn't budge. It needed me to lift it. 'Let me out!' she cried. As I listened to the *boomboomboom* of her fist on the underside of

235

the lid, remembering how she'd asked for the door of her room to be left open on her first night at Lanes End, I experienced something like the brief moments of consciousness after an anaesthetist's needle goes in, when you start to feel weightless, when you have no choice but to let go, when you know that you will be under soon, when you feel fear but also a kind of ecstasy. Freedom distilled into its purest form. You think: if only this feeling could last just a few seconds longer. Then you think: no one even knows she's here. And then: nobody in Ruby's life knows anything about you, or this place. And then: her sister will not come looking because she is in there with her. And: Lee will not confront you because he is in there with her. And: you don't know anyone around here and no one knows you. You think: there are no witnesses. You think: it's immaculate. And then with hands that no longer resemble your hands you push the hasp further down. You slip the padlock – still in your hand – through the locking eye, slowly, delicately, and click it into place. Then you kneel at the trunk and rest your cheek on the fragrant timber as though saying a silent goodbye and you say with a calm voice that does not resemble your voice: 'The lock's come down and got stuck. I'll have to remove it completely. Just hang on.'

'OK, hurry,' she said.

I found myself backing away from the trunk. When I reached the door I looked at the trunk and around at the other things and I thought: yes, this is good, this is safe. This is love. Love is something you do and I am doing it.

When I got outside and realised what I had done, there was a momentary and intense wave of nausea but it passed quickly. I closed the door gently behind me and then I felt only relief and good feelings. I felt I had acted sensibly. And then, suddenly, as though someone had pressed the mute button, there were no other thoughts in my head.

For the next forty-five minutes I was possessed. My body moved on its own. My arms swept up Ruby's things from every room and dumped them into her holdall bag. My legs knew where everything was located and carried me to it; every toiletry, cosmetic, tissue, deodorant bottle, stray red hair. My hands knew to rummage through the bathroom bin, to feel beneath and inside pillows, to clean every glass, mug, knife, fork and spoon, to strip the bedsheets. They knew to grab the big green tarp from behind the kitchen that I used to cover firewood and take it and the whole sundry lot out onto the shale and throw it into the boot of the red Mini. And then I was in the Mini and driving it bumpily through the trees, to a spot so deep in the woods that I had walked there only once before, in the days of the beard and the pebbles. And then I was taking the tarp and throwing it over the Mini like a gigantic tablecloth and securing it to the ground with stones and rocks. I checked my watch. Eleven fifty-five. Five minutes. I ran back to the cottage and gave each room a quick once-over. Despite, perhaps, the Halloween trimmings, there was no sign at all that anyone else had ever been here.

I was breathless from the run but satisfied. Serene. I decided to go meet Vic at the gate. I didn't want to risk her getting lost and stumbling across the Mini.

Her taxi appeared on the crest of the long road at five past twelve. It pulled onto the muddy triangle before the gate. Vic paid the driver and then got out, grimacing at the condition of the sludgy ground. The taxi turned around and sped off towards Wilder. She looked me up and down.

'You're a vampire.'

'Dracula, specifically,' I said. I noticed immediately that she was dressed normally. Gone were the yoga pants, the luminous orange crop top, the running shoes, the microfibre tracksuit jacket. She wore white jeans tucked into grey suede boots and a thick grey oversized jumper beneath a grey wool overcoat. Gone also was the tan and the irradiated blonde hair. Her skin was pale and her hair was back to its natural shade. She shot me a cautious smile, meant to convey shame, guilt, remorse, many millions of apologies. Tamely, I smiled back.

'I had no idea you were so into Halloween.'

'Your note said you had things you needed to say?' I said. I had no idea why I was being so brusque. Maybe seeing her again brought back some of the pain of her leaving.

'Can we please not do this here?'

'Come on.' I opened the gate and led her along the lane. Being with her again made me strangely nervous. We walked in silence.

As we approached the clearing my heart began to pound. I looked at my watch. Ruby had been locked up for over an hour. What if she had begun to panic, started screaming? I knew Victoria; she would go straight to the sound to investigate. So when we reached the shale courtyard I was relieved to hear nothing. Perhaps she'd got the screaming out of her system. Perhaps she'd given up, fallen asleep, knocked herself out. I opened the cottage side door and waited inside for Vic to enter. This was just the third time she'd set foot inside Lanes End. Her eyes widened at the mural on the wall.

'Did you do this?' she asked.

'With help.' She walked along the corridor, ducking beneath a cloud of bats suspended from the ceiling.

'Where does it end?'

'It goes everywhere.' She paused at the centre point of the corridors and looked in each direction. I looked down, to avoid her gaze, and I suddenly realised why this vampire costume made me so uneasy: it reminded me of the way Frank used to dress, all in black, like a member of the clergy.

'That cross outside. It says Daniel.'

'Yes.' Tears came into her eyes then but she managed to hold them back before they fell. 'This was going to be the nursery wasn't it,' she said marching towards it. 'Alfred's cage. Where is he?'

'He passed away.'

'What? When?'

'Last week.'

'How? What was wrong with him? I mean, they're supposed to live to thirty.'

'I don't know. I just found him in the bottom of his cage one morning.'

'Oh no.'

'What did you come here to say, Vic?'

'Can we sit down somewhere?'

I took her into the sitting room where the fire was still going. She took off her overcoat and slung it over the back of an armchair. She continued to compliment me on the cottage. She asked about the rocking chair, the books on the mantelpiece, the painting. I said it had been painted by the same friend who'd done the mural. By the time we sat down to talk properly it was twelve-thirty. I took off my cape and unbuttoned the ruffled white shirt. Victoria eyed me strangely, imploringly. She looked as though on the verge of throwing up. She broke down.

240

'Oh Dan, my life is a mess,' she said, plunging a hand into her bag and producing a pack of Kleenex. 'I should never have treated you like I did. Scott's a fraud. Life with him is a total fraud. I didn't know what I was doing back then. You were just so cold, so distant all the time, always in your workshop, always working on something, never me, never us. And there was just so much pain, I didn't know what to do with it. Every time I looked at you the pain got worse. And then there was *your* pain too, I know, and I ran from it. Scott is awful. He's wracked with insecurities. He hates his life. Hates his *body*, as if that wasn't obvious. He lives inside a prison. And I put myself in there with him, locked myself up alongside him. He thought achieving perfection was the key to escaping it. He started checking up on me when I was eating: have you counted those macros? When I was exercising: how many sets is that? When I was doing nothing: wasn't your rest day yesterday?

'I've been so depressed. Sometimes it seemed like my life was lived online. Everything stage-managed. Everything lit, filmed, refilmed, edited. It's not a life. None of that is real. I hate lifting weights. I hate feeling guilty about not lifting weights. I'm sick of always having to be pristine, always having to be perfectly put together. I don't want to eat chicken, sweet potato and broccoli every day. I hate fucking laughing yoga. I did all of that because it was something to do to take my mind to another place, a place I didn't need to think. A place away from pain. Am I making sense? Lifting and running and meditating and all of that stuff, it was like putting my mind in a jar. But it became an obsession. It was stupid. So stupid. I see that now. Oh Dan,' she said, her voice dropping an octave, 'I made a terrible mistake leaving you, the biggest of my life. I've made myself ill. But I never stopped loving you.'

She rose then to her feet and began removing her jumper. I thought she was just hot from the fire. But once the jumper was off she slipped out of the singlet beneath it too.

'Vic,' I said. She said nothing. She stood before me in just her bra and jeans. Her mouth was open slightly and she was breathing rapidly through it. There was so much anguish and longing in her expression. It called to something within me and I found it impossible not to answer. I stood up and began undressing. Frantically, I tugged and pulled at each maddening layer of the costume, stumbling, almost falling. Eventually, my hands were joined in the struggle by Vic's and we collapsed to the floor. I began pulling and twisting to get free but Vic was pushing her hand into my chest, coaxing me to lay flat on my back. I grabbed her firmly by the hips and turned her around. She sank to her hands and knees and placed her palms on the arms

242

of the chair before her for balance. After that it was a mad, blinding scramble. When I think about it now I see only a series of fire-lit, dreamlike images: Vic before me on her knees, rising over me, sliding beneath me, her eyes looking into mine with a kind of fury, and I recall nothing of the way it felt. This was not so much an act of desire or love; this was reparation, for both of us, repayment of a long-standing debt. Something the world owed us. I didn't think of Ruby, not because I had already forgotten her, but because I did not think of anything. And as I dozed off afterwards and my senses began to return, I felt a sensation of hollowness in my belly, a massive hunger such as I had never known. I felt as if some concentrated lump of toxic matter had been exorcised from my stomach, leaving a hole.

With the last spark of consciousness before exhausted sleep took me, I knew how I would fill that hole, how I would satisfy that hunger.

...

...

...

...

...

...

Ruby

...

...

...

...

...

...

Ruby

...

...

...

...

...

...

Ruby

...

...

...

...

...

...

'Who's Ruby?'

...

'You keep saying *Ruby*. Who's Ruby?'

Am I dreaming?

'Dan!'

'Ruby?'

'No, it's Victoria.'

My feet were cold. My neck was cold. But the rest of me was warm. My eyes began to open. Orange light.

Flames. Heat. The scent of varnish. Yes, this was home. Our home.

'You've been dreaming,' Victoria said. I opened my eyes now. She was sitting on the rocking chair by the fire, shrouded in a blanket. 'You kept saying *Ruby* over and over. Who's Ruby?'

Victoria's face was radiant. Evidently, she'd been watching me sleep. I looked behind her to the window, filled now with the dark blue of evening. Where had the light gone?

Then I remembered what I'd done.

'What time is it?' I said sitting upright in the armchair. Victoria brought her wristwatch to her eye and told me. Ruby had been locked up for over eight hours.

'Is something wrong?' she said.

I thought about this for a moment. I thought about Ruby out there in the freezing workshop. It was a pity but now that it was over I realised there really wasn't anything else to be done. Even if I'd successfully broken it off with Ruby and somehow got through this day, I could never have trusted her to stay away. She might've returned at any time, at any period of my life, out of the blue, to wreck everything. I couldn't have lived with that hanging over me.

'No. Everything's fine,' I said. 'Everything's going to be OK now.' I stood up and reached out a hand towards Vic. 'Come on, let's go to bed.'

I'm probably gonna be going away soon. This is what Robbie said to me earlier today. *So I may as well tell you this.* The 'this' I could've had a decent guess at; you hear things around here. Which of my theories about this strange, crumpled-up old man would be confirmed? Where was he going away to? He seemed lighter, at peace, as if he had relinquished a great and troubling burden, just decided to set it down by the roadside. Is he dying? I wondered. Or is this just the way men get when they reach a certain age? *It were me Danny,* he said. *I wrapped that scarf round Maud's neck and I wrung the life out of her. God help me.*

I slept soundly. I did not dream. I woke very early and watched Vic sleep. Her face was completely obscured by a mess of hair. Her breath was both acrid and sweet. I didn't yet know how I felt about everything. But my head was clear. And my father used to say that when you do a big thing and the next morning you have a clear head, it's a sure sign the thing was right to do. I dozed intermittently.

I was stirred by a knock. A little percussive sound of the sort the house emitted by itself from time to time. I paid it no mind and closed my eyes. But there it was again. Knock-knock. Weak. An unsure knock. I looked at Vic. She hadn't heard it. I disentangled myself from her and slipped out into the corridor. I could see nobody through the frosted glass of the side door. I went outside to investigate. I looked left and right but there was no one. Was my conscience making a late play for attention? I went back and stood at the door for a moment, in just boxers, and enjoyed the sharpness of the November air on my torso. Then I heard a couple of crunchy footsteps. They came from my left. I looked in that direction, expecting and wanting it to be one of the motorcyclists, craving now confrontation, a final showdown, an end to everything. I felt my body ready itself, pump itself up.

What I saw stopped my heart.

'Sorry if I woke you,' Ruby said, glancing down at my boxers. She sounded different. Measured, composed, transcendent in the way that characters in films are when they return to confront their nemesis at the end. It's hard to relay just how jarring this experience was for me. 'You must be Dan?' she offered her hand. I gave her mine and let it be shaken. 'Jade.'

I knew then that it was all real. Ruby was telling the truth about everything.

Everything she'd said to me or done with me had been real. There had been no reason to distrust her after all. No reason to kill her. None. Oh god, what had I done?

I had been the one all along. Me.

I was the one who was dangerous, who was mad, who couldn't be trusted.

Some instinct assumed control of my body and voice once more and enabled me to step fully onto the shale and close the door softly behind me. Whatever was about to be said I didn't want Victoria to hear.

'How can I help you?' I said.

'It's my sister Ruby. I'm assuming there's a high probability of you knowing this, but she recently got out of prison.' I nodded. 'Well she mentioned she'd got to know this guy, Dan,' she said, gesturing to me, 'while she was inside, through letters, correspondence. I understand she's been spending some time with you since she got out, here?'

'She visited me a few weeks ago to give me a painting. She's a talented artist.'

'The painting, yes. Highly skilled artist. She mentioned that, the painting.' Jade looked pained, lost.

'Is something up?'

'Well since she got out we've kept in touch every day on the phone. I haven't heard from her since the day before yesterday. It's highly unlike her. Not to check in. Not to let me know she's, you know, alive.'

'And you're worried is what you're saying?'

'Yes.'

'That something might've happened to her?' It took

every ounce of willpower I had, actual physical effort, not to allow my eyes to dart either to the workshop or the woods where I'd hidden the Mini.

'Yes. She's been worried about her ex-boyfriend coming after her. She said she was coming to spend Halloween here, with you, at this place. Really excited.'

'Really? That's weird. I've only seen her the one time and that was when she brought the picture.' Jade placed her hands on the back of her head and rotated slowly around scanning the treeline, as if she might catch a glimpse of her lost sibling wandering in the woods.

'Right.'

'Maybe she's with this ex-boyfriend?' I said. Jade snorted mirthlessly.

'Highly unlikely. Very low possibility.'

'I'm so sorry. Is there a number I can get you on if she happens to stop by again?' She had by now begun meandering forlornly away from me, edging nearer and nearer to the workshop. 'Jade?' She stooped to look through the nursery window, making a visor of her hand on the glass. She suddenly straightened up and looked at me.

'Number? Oh, no. That's all right. It doesn't sound like you can help. Thanks anyway,' she said. Then she marched quickly away, cutting a huge corner over the clearing, and disappeared up the lane. She was in such a sudden hurry to leave that she flattened one of the crosses and didn't stop to stand it back up. When she was out of sight I went to the nursery window myself and looked inside. When I saw what she'd seen I knew she knew I was lying to her.

The mural.

She'd obviously recognised her sister's artwork. She was probably already calling the police.

I was straight back into crisis management mode. I went back inside. When I looked at Victoria I suddenly felt the weight of my betrayal. But there was no time to mope around feeling sorry for myself. I had to find a way to get through this. I woke Victoria up, fed her some lie about a job I had in someone else's workshop. I had to go, basically now, and so did she, and we could pick this up later but I can't lose this job and so on. I didn't exactly stuff her clothes into her arms in a bundle but I think she took it the wrong way, judging by the wounded expression. I no longer cared. I knew now that the overpowering desire I'd felt to have her back was simply a desire for something familiar.

'Can you drop me home?' she said.

'I'm going east to Bowland, you're not on the way.'

'Well call me a cab then.'

'Right.' The conversation was so reminiscent of how things were in those last awful months together. But at the time I was too preoccupied with getting rid of her before the police turned up for it to register.

I ordered a taxi and waited with her at the gate. She stood with her arms folded, not looking in my direction, not talking, and I knew that last night we had not reunited but only made our separation more permanent. I watched her get into the car. With Victoria gone I did another sweep of the rooms for Ruby's things (I found her witch's hat hanging on a doorknob and threw it in the fire), secured the workshop with another padlock and pulled the curtains to in the nursery. I was nervous about the Mini but there was nothing I could do about that before they came. I went to make the bed Vic and I had slept in, but thought it would be better to leave it unmade. Then I showered and dressed and sat at the kitchen table and waited for them to come. There was still Halloween stuff everywhere. Buckets of sweets, rotting pumpkins, decorations. They might ask if I had guests. I couldn't say yes, there was nobody I could name to corroborate. I would have to lie and say I spent Halloween alone, that I did all of this for myself. It would seem odd. I would have to have my wits about me. I spent a few hours running through each possible line of questioning and shoring up my nerves. And then they came.

It was half-past three and the light was already fading. I heard the patrol car roll onto the shale and then two doors open and close. I went out the side door to meet them. Two uniformed officers, both female. One short, one tall.

'Afternoon sir,' the short one said.

'Afternoon. How can I help you?' The tall officer pressed her hat onto her head and wandered off towards the workshop.

'Is this your property sir?' the short officer said. The tall one began peering into the windows of the workshop one by one.

'Yes. I'm the owner. Can I ask what this is about?' I watched the tall officer move away from the workshop towards the garage.

'Are you acquainted with a Miss Ruby Holland sir?'

'Yes. I know her. Her sister was by earlier today asking after her too. What's going on here please?' The tall officer disappeared behind the garage.

'Miss Holland has been reported missing. We're trying to ascertain her last known whereabouts. Has she been here recently?'

'She came here about a month ago to give me a painting.'

'A painting?'

'Yes, of me. She was in prison until recently. We used to write letters to each other, through a programme called –'

'– and you haven't seen her since?'

'No. She only came here that one time. Is she in trouble? Is she all right?'

'Do you mind if we have a look inside your property

252

sir?' The tall officer reappeared from the gap between the cottage and the workshop. She took her place along-side her shorter and evidently senior colleague.

'Of course not, come in.' I showed them inside. I was confident there wasn't anything incriminating for them to see inside the cottage. But as I followed them from room to room I couldn't control the furious beating of my heart.

'Is this the painting?' the short officer asked.

'Yes,' I said, folding my arms to hide the violent shudders seizing my whole body. The tall one ran her finger across the spines of the books on the mantelpiece. They did not enquire about the Halloween decorations. But on their way out I clocked a little nod of acknowl-edgement between them as they each saw the mural, which stretched, still unfinished, from the nursery all the way along the corridor. Back outside, the tall one whispered something into her colleague's ear and then walked away muttering into her radio. 'Mind if we have a quick look inside your outbuildings sir?'

Think! Quick!

'Oh, I only use them for storage. I keep my old tools locked up in there. And some antiques, valuable antiques in fact some of them. I don't have much call to go in there these days. In fact I don't think I quite remember where the key is.'

'I'd appreciate if you could locate it sir.'

'Right, yes. Let me have a look for you. One minute.' I went inside and stood in the kitchen. I could not generate a single productive thought. After a reasonable length of time I went back outside with a ring of keys in my hand and the actual key to the padlock in my pocket. 'It must be one of these,' I said, and proceeded to try them one by one. After a few fails the tall officer went to the boot of the patrol car and produced a pair of bolt cutters. She marched towards me.

'Allow me sir,' she said in a surprisingly high-pitched voice.

'Hey, what do you think you're doing?' I protested, moving to block her way. 'You can't just destroy my property. You can't just barge your way in without my permission.'

'Sir, we can replace your padlock. Believe me it will be far better for everyone if you allow us to go inside now. Mostly, missing persons cases are solved within twenty-four hours or they're not solved at all. All we're doing is ruling out certain possibilities as quickly as possible. We don't want to have to obtain a warrant and come back when we could be using our time to investigate other leads.' I thought about my options for a moment. But then realised I had none.

'No, I'm sorry, this is ridiculous. I won't allow it. I don't know what possibilities you need to rule out but you're wasting your time here. And if you continue to harass me like this I'll have to make a complaint.' The tall officer turned to look at her superior who signalled for her to stand down with an almost imperceptible shake of her head. Then she lowered the bolt cutters and walked back to the car.

'Have it your way. Thank you for your time sir.' The shorter officer touched the rim of her hat, got back into the car and drove off.

For some time after they'd driven away I stared at the cloud of dust the car had kicked up. I watched it swirl and drift and eventually diffuse into nothing. And then I watched the space the car had occupied, unthinking, unmoving. And then, as though the idea had been waiting the whole time in the hidden chambers of my mind, I knew what to do.

I looked at my watch. Ten past four. The sun would set in an hour and a half. I had to wait for darkness to carry out the second part of my plan, they might be watching me from the woods. But it was already dark enough to do the first part, if I was careful.

I reversed the Transporter into the gap between the cottage and the workshop, obscuring any view of the door from the lane, opened the van's back double-doors and went into the workshop. I crept slowly over to the trunk, listening intently. There was no sound. I knelt before it and pressed my ear to the lid – perhaps she was asleep – but I could hear not a thing. The task at hand was grisly but I told myself – repeating it like a mantra – *it's only a trunk, it's only a trunk, it's only a trunk*, and I manoeuvred it, via a combination of pushing and dragging, out onto the shale. Then, with some difficulty, and trying to ignore the hard-soft sound of Ruby's limbs knocking against the sides, I hoisted it up into the back of the Transporter. *It's only a trunk, it's only a trunk.* I managed to do all of this without looking at it directly. If I'd looked I'd have thought of what lay inside and my resolve would've collapsed. I slammed the Transporter's doors shut and went back into the workshop to arrange the remaining trunks so they would appear how the tall officer had observed them through the window, marvelling and sort of inwardly convulsing at my own ability to think so clearly. I took the laptop from the drawer behind the Chinese screen and put it on the driver's seat. It wasn't safe to leave that lying around, it would have to go too. Then I resecured the workshop door with the padlock and went inside the cottage to wait for sunset.

I spent the intervening time alternating between sitting on the edge of the unmade bed and standing in the bay window looking out across the clearing. Already some sort of grief was taking hold of me. Echoes of things she'd said, images of her painting, cooking, reading aloud to me. As the sky darkened I looked up at the emergent North Star. *If you can see that you're not lost,* she once said. Well I could see it now and I was completely lost.

At quarter to six I grabbed a cap and jacket and went out to the Transporter. There wasn't a sound. Winter was near and there wasn't a single sign of life from the woods. No buzzing insects or rustling birdlife. Everything was asleep or elsewhere. It was cold. I could see my breath. Just before I climbed into the driver's seat I patted my pocket to check for both padlock keys, the one for the workshop and the one for the trunk. I rolled along the lane slowly, not wanting to jibe the trunk, not wanting to hear its mass scrape across the metal floor and clatter into the sides of the van. The police had left the gate open and I drove straight out to the road. I went left, east, towards Bowland, away from Wilder. I drove past Gray's farm and The Lighthouse pub. As I ascended the crest of a gentle peak a pair of headlights, a couple of hundred metres behind me, flashed in my rear-view and caught my attention. Was someone following me? Of course not. I was feeling, understandably, paranoid. I'm certain everyone committing a crime, whether it's swapping price stickers in the supermarket or transporting a body, feels they're either being followed or watched. I continued on, along the road Ruby had herself driven in the opposite direction to get to me, towards Bowland Forest. It was only once I had breached the treeline and got out of the open that I felt safe. I kept a close eye on my rear-view as I followed the snaking lane through the forest. After a while I realised the headlights had disappeared. And when I rounded a few more bends I felt sure I was in the clear. I took the turn off to Bowland Reservoir and killed my headlights. The road here was extremely narrow and gravelly, more of a track than a road. I took it slowly, leaning forward over the steering wheel to try to pick out the track's edges. Eventually, I reached a point where I could see the water, black and placid, a mirror for the stars. But I was not near enough to do what I came to do. I rolled the Transporter off the road to get closer and then turned off the engine. For a few moments I remained inside assessing the terrain between the front of the van and the water: a strip of moonlit scrubland which rose to a manicured grassy lip. I got out, taking the laptop with me, and went around the back of the Transporter. It would be necessary to put the laptop inside the trunk, having two separate things floating around out there represented a far greater risk. My hands were shaking uncontrollably as I reached into my pocket for the key. I still remember the sound of the key rattling like a cup and saucer in an earthquake as I struggled to align it with the lock. But suddenly I felt it slide in, and then I was turning it and pulling it loose and pushing open the lid.

She was curled up, foetal, as though she'd simply

decided to take a nap. For a split second I thought she was OK. *Just sleeping*, I thought. *Peacefully sleeping.* But that was only upon first glance. When I looked closer, at her fingertips, at the markings on the underside of the lid, at her face, screwed up grotesquely, it was obvious she was dead. Gingerly, I reached inside and touched her cheek. I felt an overwhelming desire to massage her facial muscles into a more relaxed pose, as though this would somehow bring her peace. She was cold. I rubbed and rubbed her cheeks but I could not do anything about her eyes, which were glued shut into nasty little asterisks, or her distended mouth. I retched up caustic bile. Some went inside the trunk but mostly I got it on myself. I reached inside the trunk with both arms and pulled her heavy limp torso out and held her in my lap.

I think even before I heard the slamming of car doors or the sound of my megaphoned name, or saw the interior of the Transporter light up blue, I had decided to give up.

Lucy, I won't give you a blow-by-blow account of my trial. Now that *is* something you can find online. But I do wish to dispel a couple of myths. The press observed that I sat 'stony faced' throughout the proceedings. That isn't true. They said I showed 'no reaction' when the judge delivered his summing-up. Lies. They said those things I suppose in order to paint an appropriate picture, to sell their chosen narrative, like a movie trailer.

Court was a circus. Wading through the scrum of newspaper photographers detonating their flashes and the TV journalists with their microphones pointed at me like bayonets was a degrading farce. People think the hand in front of the face is to avoid giving them a clear photograph but it's really to protect your eyes from the flashes. I didn't know why my trial had commanded so much media attention until one of the guards showed me a newspaper. HOUSE OF HORRORS, the front page shouted, with blurred black-and-white photographs of Lanes End dressed up for Halloween: the line of hosepipe nooses, the tools lined up on the tea tray, the 'deadly chemicals', the 'cemetery' out front, the jack-o'-lanterns leading to the workshop. FACTORY OF DEATH, the papers cried. They referred to my mango wood trunks as 'coffins'. 'Ready-made' read the caption beneath the photo of them lined up in the workshop, lids open like hungry mouths.

I suppose the photographs were leaked or sold to the press by the police. There can be no other explanation. They made me famous, a Halloween monster. During my first interrogation they kept asking me over and over about the rosewood crosses on the lawn: *Where are the others? Where have you hidden them? Who's Alfred?*

Who's Ivy? Tell us where you've buried them. You'll get a shorter sentence if you tell us. If I was myself I'd have laughed at them. But my arms were still tingling with the feeling of Ruby's limp body in the back of the Transporter. I could still smell the sweat-soaked polyester of her costume wedding dress. I could still see her open mouth and her scrunched-up eyes which I had tried and failed to prise open for one last look. I sat there in the tiny cold interrogation room with my hands open in the same position they were when they found me and pulled me away from her. Without me to hold her she had folded over the edge of the trunk like a ragdoll. *How many others are there? Tell us!* They seized on other things too: my inventory of supplies – the bleach, the razor blades, the electrical tape, the giant compost maker out back – for which I could offer no reasonable explanation. *Just what were you planning, you sick bastard?*

The pictures made it real. They were displayed on a screen in the courtroom. Wide shots of the exterior of the cottage, the clearing, the lane, the driveway, the shale courtyard. Shots of the inside of the workshop, scattered with little yellow evidence markers and arrows indicating the direction in which I'd hauled the trunk across the ground, of the tools hanging in their slots on the back wall. Shots of the laptop (which, later, they analysed, finding all of the Inbox Inmate correspondence).

They held up the copies of the true-crime books in my collection – *In Cold Blood*, *The Executioner's Song*, *Helter-Skelter* – and said they demonstrated an 'obsession with violence'. They ignored the others. They also passed around the claw hammer, which was still in my bedside drawer, as further evidence of my 'violent nature'. It was the close-up shots of the trunk – of Ruby's body, of her red hair mingling with the sawdust on the floor of the van, of the blood marks inside the trunk where she had clawed her fingernails off – which had the greatest impact. She had died of panic, essentially, had suffered a massive heart attack.

Though I confessed everything to him, Mr Bainbridge – whom I had appointed as my solicitor advocate because I could think of no one else – felt he had a duty to 'save my life' and persuaded me to accept the lesser charge of perverting the course of justice but to let him try to get the murder charge dropped. He would argue that Ruby's death was in fact an accident, that her being locked inside the trunk was some sort of horseplay which had then gone tragically wrong. Yes, granted I had been caught attempting to dispose of the evidence – and for that we were offering no defence – but I had not intended to harm Ruby and we were in fact in love. The wigged and gowned prosecution barrister had an easy time swatting that argument away: the defendant had left Miss Holland to freeze in his workshop while he made love to his former partner had he not? What kind of love is that? Bainbridge had no riposte.

The trial passed mostly in a blur. I paid very little attention to what the lawyers were saying most of the time; I knew I would be convicted, and I knew that I deserved to be. I wanted to be. Nothing the justice system could do to me was strong enough, I thought. I cursed the fact that our society no longer permitted public floggings, stonings, humiliations. I wanted to hurt. I wanted to die.

My mind faltered. One day I thought I saw Ruby's ghost in the public gallery. She looked murderously down at me. Her hair wasn't red any more, it was black with a streak of white. Did death rob a person of their colour? An urge to get up and call out to her, to tell her I loved her and I was sorry came over me. My legs began to move involuntarily and the chain between my cuffed ankles jangled softly. Bat-eared Bainbridge, seated beside me, heard this and as I went to stand he put his hand on my thigh to stop me. He followed my gaze upwards to the gallery and he whispered, in the same tone of voice the nurses at Jerusalem adopted when they spoke to my mother: 'That's Ruby's sister, Daniel.'

I wish he had let me keep that particular delusion.

Ruby's little dark book turned out to be, of course, her

diary. She had maintained it until the very end. The prosecution read aloud from it. It confirmed what I had known to be true ever since Jade turned up at Lanes End. She wasn't behind the vandalised shed, the break-in, Alfred's murder, the power cut, or any of that stuff. She was genuinely fearful for her safety, for her life. She really did believe Lee had tracked her down to Wilder, just as she had told me, a belief which proved well founded when Lee himself took the stand to describe how he'd been staking out Lanes End for weeks, how he'd taken a room in a B&B in Wilder-on-Sea, how he'd written Ruby a short drunken letter one night and hand-delivered it and how he'd followed me to Bowland in his car and called the police on the way and how he'd pointed out where I'd gone off-road in the forest and how he watched as I was cuffed and put in the back of the patrol car and driven away.

Ruby's journal also explained why she didn't want the police involved after the break-in. She had been driving Jade's Mini illegally, using her twin's driving licence in case she was ever pulled over. Having just been released from prison she herself was without a valid licence or insurance and she feared the misdemeanour might have landed her back inside. She felt she couldn't tell me this at the time. She wanted to seem 'normal' and hated the fact that her conviction had erected a 'wall of misgiving' around her. A wall which, so the journal narrated, she had resolved to dismantle stone by stone. The journal revealed other things too. She was never in cahoots with Jade. There was never any plot to hurt me, or avenge the psychic hurt I'd inflicted upon her. The journal made no mention of the two helmeted men. Hearing Ruby's words spoken out loud filled me with rage. This was a violation. These private thoughts were never intended to be heard. But there was a point to the readings: to cast me as jealous, possessive, controlling. 'I will have to be patient,' Ruby wrote. 'He questioned me at the pub last night when some young guy bought me a drink. He still doesn't trust me.' The prosecution used the journal to insinuate that Ruby was afraid of me. They implied for example that the steak knife, which she had lifted from her sister's house and kept with her as protection from Lee, was intended as protection from me. 'I see him watching me sometimes when I'm on the phone to Jade,' she had written. 'I wish I felt safe enough to tell him every thought that's in my head but I don't. Not yet. There are moments when I'm not sure I really know him at all. He goes all quiet and stares into space and I feel like it's better just to leave him be. I suppose we've both got a lot of dark stuff to work through. For now I'm afraid Jade will have to continue bearing the brunt of my craziness. Sorry sis! But what are twins for?'

Two witnesses were called to give evidence relating

to my character. Max Gray and his eldest son. Gray told the court that I was a strange individual, that I was a loner, that I didn't associate with others. He implied my isolation went further than a desire for privacy and that people were suspicious of me. Gray said that I was only ever seen once in the local pub, with the victim, and on said occasion I had behaved strangely, keeping the victim barricaded in a corner all night by the fruit machine. He wasn't there that night, Gray admitted, but his son was and he had told Gray how he'd watched me all night from the other side of the bar. His son had bought the victim a shot to see how I'd react. And how did he react, the prosecuting lawyer asked Gray. By all accounts not well, Gray said.

Gray's son's main beef with me was that I had been accepting his father's meagre deliveries of eggs and milk for months without paying. This was a shock to me. I had assumed they were merely surplus and being delivered to me gratis as payment was never discussed and they just kept on coming without my ever requesting them in the first place. I would have gladly paid had he asked. But Gray's son took my 'refusal to pay' as a major affront to the honour of his father who was too meek and drunk to defend it himself. So he and his younger brother had 'played a few tricks' on me with the intention first of inciting an attack of conscience and thereafter, when it seemed my conscience was either misplaced or nonexistent, simply 'to get our own back'. Bainbridge said the Gray boys' acts – which, let's face it, he said, were a bit more than mere tricks and they should be thankful his client wasn't bringing charges of his own against them – had brought an air of terror to Lanes End, which should surely, to some extent, provide at least a little mitigation for his client's actions in the lead-up to Miss Holland's accidental death? The prosecuting lawyer had nothing to say to this, not because Bainbridge had dumbfounded or outmanoeuvred him in any way, but simply because the writing was already on the wall: I was guilty and his work was done.

I spent the last days of the trial thinking about suicide. At night I tried to devise a way of doing it there in my cell before the verdict, which I didn't care about. But I could never find a way: I would have to wait until prison. Once there I would network; there must be loads of guys, I thought, who knew how to get things like that done.

On the morning of the closing speeches and the summing-up, Victoria came to court. The verdict was to be delivered in the afternoon. She shuffled along the front row of the public gallery in a white summer dress with pink flowers, holding her swollen belly with both hands. The people already seated stood one by one in a Mexican wave to make way for her, displaying that special, fevered kind of reverence reserved only for heavily pregnant women. She took her seat and fixed my gaze. I looked at her and through the closing speeches I tried to decode the silent message she was sending. A short while later, as Mr Justice A. Wills launched into his grandiloquent summing-up speech – written so floridly no doubt for the benefit of the national journalists present – I felt an odd kind of peace. Nothing could ever take away the hate I now reserved for myself or fill the hole left by Ruby's death, but seeing the new life Victoria carried on her front gave me hope.

'... each man kills the thing he loves ...' The judge recited part of the famous verse, and as he condemned me I could not stop a smile. All had come to an end and yet here I was at the beginning of something. I felt a renewed desire to go on living.

***

Gordon told me Robbie's been transferred to another prison. *Nice guy, but he'd fallen in with some real low-lifes,* he said, stroking his white stubble. *Serious guys Danny. Organised. Not men you mix with if you want to do your time quietly. We found a mobile phone in his mattress. We think he's been moving contraband for months, possibly over a year, we don't know yet. I don't know what got into him. I probably shouldn't be telling you this.* He loitered awkwardly at my door for a while.

The wife loved the mirror frame by the way. Loved it. Did she know half the furniture in her house was hand-crafted by a convicted murderer, I joked. He laughed. *Not long now is it?* he said, referring to my release next month. November. *What'll you do?*

Most screws are vindictive thugs. But Gordon's all right. Not saying I'll miss him, but he's not bad for a screw.

I've been thinking about Lanes End. All along I was certain I'd never set foot there again but now I'm not so sure. I once had a premonition the place would end up as a tomb, destined to lie forever uninhabited, home to ghosts and the echoes of love from a time long past. At the time I thought of Vic. But of course – of course! – it is Ruby's tomb. Perhaps it's right that I should go back and wait for a glimpse of my demon bride in her polyester wedding dress.

Lucy, your whole life I've been behind bars. Locked away in this room that I refuse to call a cell. I've sometimes wallowed in self-pity and I've sometimes cried – sixteen years is a long time – but mostly I've lived with my bow pointed not at the rocks but at the horizon, towards the future. Because of you.

I've thought of you every day. When you turned four I imagined you in a little grey pinafore ready for school. When you turned eleven the pinafore was replaced by a blouse and tie. And now that you've turned sixteen and have exercised your right to contact me without your mother's permission (I can't blame her keeping us apart all these years, not after what she saw, not after everything I've put her through), I picture you as an angel. My guardian angel. You saved my life (do you think that was your mother's intention in court?) and I don't know how to thank you. I don't know how to adequately show you how much I love you. I've made you this little gift but it doesn't come close to saying what I want to say. I hope you'll let me do that in person one day.

I've decided. Just now. I'm going back to Lanes End. I'm going to gut the cottage, start again from scratch. I'm going to rebuild. I'm going to make a space there just for you.

That's where you'll find me.

I'll write again soon.

Affectionately yours

Dad

ACKNOWLEDGEMENTS

Firstly, I'd like to thank my agent – the great Eve White. My association with Eve goes back to the summer of 2012 and it is testament not only to her patience with a young author finding his voice, but to her guiding wisdom and loyalty that we are now – seven years later – finally publishing our first novel together. Eve's enduring faith in my talent has been and continues to be a source of immense pride and motivation, and I look forward to sharing much more success with her in the future.

I must also mention and thank Eve's assistant, Ludo Cinelli. A smarter, more affable and astute operator you are unlikely to find. (Thanks also to Ludo's predecessor Kitty Walker, from whom I learned so much.)

'Gratitude' does a lousy job of describing my feelings towards my editor, Cecily Gayford. Simply put, without Cecily this book wouldn't exist. Cecily had a clear vision for *This Little Dark Place* and the courage to take a chance on me. I hope I executed her plan well and that she is as proud of the finished product as I am. The biggest compliment I can pay Cecily is that working with her has made me a far better writer. I'm forever grateful, to her, and to everyone at Serpent's Tail.

Thanks to my friend Charlotte Marriage for agreeing to meet me on a cold December evening in South Kensington to talk about prison life (*note to potential employers: Charlotte had previously worked with offenders and has never – to my knowledge – been incarcerated herself*).

Thanks to my dad for showing me his carpentry tools in his freezing garage on Christmas Day while I took pictures and notes on my phone.

Thanks, and love, to my mum and my sister who came to London and picked me up when the world had dished out a serious drubbing. From the ashes of that dreadful winter came this novel.

Special thanks also to my dear friend and fellow bibliophile Carol Quearney, from whose brilliant mind I steal liberally and shamelessly.

Above all, thank you Tarryn, for your patience, your love, and your constancy. I hope you're proud of me.